3

KICKBACK

ALSO BY DAMIEN BOYD

As the Crow Flies
Head in the Sand

DAMIEN BOYD
KICKBACK

THOMAS & MERCER

Text copyright © 2015 Damien Boyd
All rights reserved.

Published by Thomas & Mercer, Seattle

www.apub.com

Amazon, the Amazon logo, and Thomas & Mercer are trademarks of Amazon.com, Inc., or its affiliates.

ISBN-13: 978-1477821053
ISBN-10: 1477821058

Cover concept by Littera Designs
Cover created by bürosüd° München, www.buerosued.de

Library of Congress Control Number: 2014947407

Printed in the United States of America

For Joy

Prologue

Race days were the best days. They made it all worthwhile. All the feeding and mucking out; the grooming and tack cleaning; the early mornings and late nights. And then there was the relentless training; all day, every day, round and round the gallops in all weathers.

Yes, it was all about race days. And the prospect, the hope, of a winner. There had not been many in recent months, but he knew one day it would be his turn to punch the air as he crossed the line, eight lengths clear of the field. That was his dream. That and being led into the Winner's Enclosure, the crowd cheering and clapping. Better still, on board his beloved Westbrook Warrior.

For now, though, it was his job to do the mucking out. And race days made for an early start.

He was always at work at least an hour before anyone else, but then he lived at the yard in an old static caravan. It was a little too close to the muckheap for comfort, perhaps, but it was free and he was near the horses.

His horses.

The season was a few weeks old and today was to be the second outing for Westbrook Warrior. Two miles and seven furlongs over the hurdles in the 3.10 p.m. at Taunton. The Charles Hedges Handicap Hurdle. He had checked the odds the night before and the Warrior was evens favourite. Not only that but rain was forecast, making for good to soft ground. Perfect.

Surely he must win today?

He had fed the horses and was skipping out the worst of the muck while they were eating. All except Westbrook Warrior, of course. No one went in the Warrior's stable when he was eating.

He paused for a moment to listen to the crunching of the racehorse cubes. There was something comforting about the sound of horses eating.

By 5 a.m. he had skipped out the horses racing that day and had a wheelbarrow full of muck and shavings. It was still dark and raining hard, so he had been putting off the dash to the muckheap. He pushed the heavy wheelbarrow along the front of the stables, sheltering under the canopy, and paused at the end to switch on the outside light on the corner of the barn.

The first blow struck him on the back of the head, just above and behind his right ear. The noise was deafening. Like a shotgun blast going off right by his head. He felt the bones of his skull cracking and his teeth bite deep into his tongue. Blood filled his mouth, causing him to cough and splutter. It dribbled down his chin but there was no pain. He braced himself, but it never came.

He dropped to his knees and slumped forward over the wheelbarrow, face down in the muck and straw. He heard footsteps and turned his head to look up. A figure was moving in the darkness.

The second blow hit him on the forehead above his left eye. It was louder than the first. He fell back onto the concrete plinth in front of the stables. He could smell urine and hear the rain running in the gutter in front of him. Blood began pouring down his forehead into his eyes.

He heard the familiar sound of the horses eating their haylage. Loud at first. Then it began to fade away.

He didn't hear the third blow.

Or the fourth.

Chapter One

'What shall we drink to?'

'Good question, Jane.' Dixon raised his pint glass in his right hand. 'How about living to fight another day?'

'I'll drink to that,' said Roger Poland.

'Me too,' replied Jane Winter.

They touched glasses in the middle of the table and then each took a large swig of beer.

'You really shouldn't be drinking that,' said Jane, frowning at Dixon.

'Yes, Mother.'

Detective Inspector Nick Dixon had discharged himself from hospital earlier that day, following surgery to remove a fish filleting knife from his left shoulder two days before. His arm was still in a sling and he was topped up with painkillers, which made the perfect cocktail with a pint of Kingfisher. He was enjoying a celebratory meal in his favourite curry house, The Zalshah in Burnham-on-Sea, with Detective Constable Jane Winter and the senior pathologist from Musgrove Park Hospital, Dr Roger Poland.

'So, you two are a couple, then?' asked Poland.

'The grapevine's been working overtime,' said Dixon.

'Who told you?' asked Jane.

'Can't remember. It was weeks ago.'

'Weeks?'

'Most people think we started seeing each other before we actually did,' said Dixon.

'Everyone enjoys a bit of gossip, don't they?' said Poland. 'Police officers are no different.'

'Worse, if anything,' said Dixon.

'How's the arm?'

'It'll be fine, or so they tell me. It missed the important stuff, apparently. I've got a few internal stitches and some Tramadol to keep me going.'

'Tramadol and Kingfisher?' Poland turned to Jane. 'He'll be asleep before the main course arrives.'

'All the more for us,' replied Jane.

The restaurant was filling up by the time their starters arrived. It was popular, even on a Tuesday night.

'I'm still pissed off I missed the carnival. I've not seen it since 1995 and the first chance I get to go, I'm in bloody hospital,' said Dixon.

'There's always next year,' said Jane.

'If you live that long. You've only been here a few months and you've almost been shot and then got yourself stabbed.'

'Thanks for that, Roger. You've cheered me up no end.'

'My pleasure.'

Jane was watching Dixon tucking into his seekh kebab starter. 'Better than hospital food?' she asked.

'Don't get me started on that. I'm sure they do their best, but . . .'

'Don't look at me,' said Poland. 'It's not something my patients usually complain about.'

Their laughter was drowned out by a commotion at a table at the back of the restaurant. Dixon heard raised voices and breaking glass. He turned to see lager pouring off the table onto the floor. Two waiters were already in attendance, one clearing up the broken glass and the other attempting to calm the situation. The diners were seated, two on the fixed bench seat with their backs to the wall, the third sitting opposite them on a wicker backed dining chair. Dixon watched while one waiter cleared up the spilt lager and the other fetched a replacement pint.

'Relax, you're off duty,' said Poland.

'Off sick,' said Jane.

Dixon turned back to Jane and Roger Poland. They were sitting on the bench seat opposite Dixon, who had his back to the restaurant.

'Just keep an eye on them, will you? It's a bit early to be that pissed.'

By 9 p.m. Dixon was finishing off his chicken tikka biriani. Jane and Roger Poland had finished picking at the remains of various dishes in the middle of the table and the waiters had begun clearing the empty dishes away. The conversation had ranged from forensic entomology and decomposition rates to the anatomy of gunshot and blast injuries. Dixon had noticed some strange looks from the diners sitting at the next table.

He had also been keeping an eye on the table at the back of the restaurant, looking over his shoulder at various intervals throughout the evening, much to Jane's annoyance. The three diners had been quiet for the last hour, except for the occasional outburst from the young man with short dark hair sitting with his back to the wall. He was opposite an empty chair. To his right sat a young woman and opposite her, an older man. All three were dressed casually, the younger man wearing a white polo shirt and black jeans. On the floor to his left was a brown leather jacket. He had a tattoo on

3

his left forearm and was well tanned. Dixon could see that he was becoming agitated again.

'Recognise him, Jane?' asked Dixon, looking over his shoulder.

'No.'

'What about the others?'

Jane shook her head.

'No.'

The younger man suddenly lurched across the table and grabbed the older man by the collar of his jacket. He pulled him forward over the table, sending drinks and plates crashing to the floor. The woman stood up and began screaming. The younger man threw a punch, which missed. Dixon watched the waiters trying to calm the situation. The diners at the adjacent table stood up and were escorted to the bar area at the front of the restaurant by the manager. Dixon could hear shouting and swearing.

'Right, that's it.'

He stood up.

'If it gets out of hand, Jane, call it in.'

'Your shoulder . . .'

Dixon walked to the back of the restaurant. The manager, Ravi, saw him coming and instructed the waiters to leave the table. The younger man stood up and turned to face Dixon.

'Who the fuck are you?'

'A fellow diner trying to enjoy a quiet meal with friends.'

'Well, fuck off then.'

'And a Detective Inspector in the Avon and Somerset Police.' Dixon dropped his warrant card onto the table. 'Now, sit down.'

'Make me,' said the younger man, looking at Dixon's arm in a sling.

'I have staff for that. One phone call from my colleague over there and they'll be here before you can say lamb pasanda.'

The younger man hesitated. He looked at the older man, then the woman and then back to Dixon. He sat down. Dixon sat on the empty chair opposite him. The older man spoke first.

'Are you the officer that got stabbed the other day?'

'How did you guess?'

The older man turned back to the younger man. 'This is the guy that got that murderer . . . the beheadings . . .'

'That was you?' asked the younger man.

'It was.'

'I read about that on the plane home.'

'Home from where?' asked Dixon.

'Afghanistan.'

'Soldier?'

'The Rifles.'

'Are you home for good?'

'Compassionate leave. My brother's funeral.'

'I'm sorry to hear that. What's your name?'

The older man answered.

'His name's Jon Woodman. I'm his father, Tom, and this is my daughter, Natalie.'

Dixon turned to Ravi, who was standing by the table. 'Another round of drinks here, please, Ravi. Stick it on my tab. And you can tell that lot they can sit down.'

'Thanks. What's your name?' asked Tom Woodman.

'Nick Dixon. Tell me what happened to your son.'

'Noel. He was killed by a horse. Kicked . . .'

'No, he fucking wasn't!' screamed Jon. He tried to stand up but lost his balance and fell back into his seat. 'I've had enough of this.' He reached down, picked up his leather jacket and slid along the bench seat. Then he stormed out of the restaurant.

Dixon turned to Tom Woodman. 'What was that all about?'

'He's got it into his head Noel was murdered.'

'Murdered?' asked Dixon.

'It's nonsense. Really. He was a groom at a racing yard and went in a stable with a stallion.'

'He was going to be a jockey,' said Natalie.

'Has there been a post mortem?'

'Yes. Last week. Head injuries. He was kicked.'

'I'm sorry to hear that,' said Dixon.

'He knew the risks.'

'And he loved the horses,' said Natalie.

'When's the funeral?'

'Friday.'

Dixon looked up. Jane was standing by the table.

'Everything OK?'

'Yes, I think so,' said Dixon, standing up. He turned to Tom Woodman. 'I'll leave you to it. Let me know if there is anything I can do.'

'Thank you,' replied Tom Woodman.

Dixon sat back down at his table with Jane and Roger Poland.

'What's the story, then?' asked Poland.

'Father, son and daughter. The son is home from Afghanistan for his brother's funeral.'

'And the row?'

'The son thinks his brother was murdered. He's had a few beers and got a bit carried away, that's all.'

'What happened, do we know?' asked Jane.

'He was kicked by a horse, from what I can gather. Mean anything to you, Roger?'

'Yes, it does. It was at a small racing yard near Spaxton. The new lad, James Davidson, did the PM. It was fairly straightforward, I think.'

Dixon nodded.

Ravi appeared with the sweet menu. He handed one each to Dixon, Jane and Roger Poland.

'On the house, Mr Dixon.'

⌣

It was 10.30 p.m. before the Tramadol and Kingfisher finally took effect. Dixon was fast asleep in the back of a taxi on his way back to his cottage in Brent Knoll, his head resting on Jane's shoulder. Roger Poland had taken a cab back to Taunton.

'C'mon, wake up,' said Jane, digging Dixon in the ribs. 'We're home.'

Jane helped Dixon out of the taxi.

'You got any money?'

'Don't look at me, I've only just got out of hospital,' replied Dixon.

He left Jane paying for the cab and opened the front door to be greeted by a very excited white Staffordshire terrier.

'Hello, matey.' Dixon knelt down and put his good arm around Monty. Jane appeared behind them.

'I'll give him five minutes in the field,' she said.

'Thanks.'

Dixon went upstairs to his bedroom. He closed the curtains, threw his jacket on the floor and lay on the bed. He was asleep before Jane got back with Monty.

⌣

The mix of painkillers and alcohol made for deep but fitful sleep, broken by vivid dreams and hot sweats. Dixon saw a blade glinting in the moonlight and a severed head in the sand. It was always the same. It felt as if he was lapsing into unconsciousness rather than falling asleep, but when he woke up and checked the time, it was only five or ten minutes later than the previous occasion. It was not the night's sleep he had been hoping for.

He was dozing when he became aware of a dog growling. It took him a moment to recognise that he was not dreaming. He sat up and could make out the silhouette of Monty sitting on the end of the bed. He was staring at the curtains, his head tipped to one side.

'What is it, boy?'

Dixon listened. He could hear voices outside in the road. He got out of bed, still fully clothed. Jane was stirring.

'What is it?' she asked.

'Voices. Outside.'

'What's the time?'

Dixon picked up his alarm clock and turned it to the light from the window, such as it was.

'It's 3 a.m., for heaven's sake.'

He opened the curtains a crack and peered out.

'Uniform. What the hell do they want?'

'What makes you think they're looking for us?'

There was a knock at the door.

'That,' said Dixon.

Monty jumped off the bed and raced downstairs, barking as he went. Dixon followed. He opened the front door. It was PC Cole.

'Sorry to bother you, Sir. Chief Inspector Bateman has been trying to get hold of you. Your phone must be switched off?'

'It is. What's up?'

'We have a situation at a house in Pawlett, Sir, and the inspector was hoping you might be able to attend.'

'A situation?'

'An armed siege.'

'What am I supposed . . . ?'

8

'The gunman has been asking to speak to you, Sir.'

'Me?'

'Yes, Sir.'

'Who is it, do we know?'

'No, Sir. We've come over from Cheddar to pick you up.'

'Get on the radio and find out, will you? I'll be out in a minute.'

Dixon closed the front door and ran upstairs. Jane was getting dressed.

'Did you hear that?'

'I was listening at the top of the stairs. I wonder what's . . .'

'We'll soon find out. Help me put this on,' said Dixon, throwing a thick blue pullover onto the bed. He began taking his left arm out of the sling.

'Leave your arm in the sling and put the jumper over the top,' said Jane.

She helped Dixon put the pullover on and then helped him into his coat.

'C'mon, let's get going. You stay here, matey,' said Dixon, leaving Monty sitting on the sofa.

They got into the back of the panda car.

'Well?'

'His name's Jon Woodman, Sir.'

'Who the hell is Jon Woodman?' asked Jane.

'He's a soldier home from Afghanistan who thinks his brother's been murdered,' said Dixon.

PC Cole turned the panda car around and sped out of Brent Knoll towards the A38.

Turn the bloody siren off, Constable,' said Dixon.

Once out on the A38, Cole accelerated hard. They crossed the motorway roundabout without noticeably slowing and accelerated again towards Highbridge. It was a bright moonlit night. Dixon could see the stars in the night sky but spent most the short journey watching the speedometer over PC Cole's shoulder.

'Take it slow over the bridge, will you?'

'Yes, Sir.'

Jane shook her head and smiled.

They slowed to forty miles an hour over Bristol Bridge and then accelerated through the town. Dixon watched the blue lights flashing in the shop windows, recognising the fishing tackle shop as they raced past. They crossed the small roundabout on the wrong side of the road and accelerated hard on the long straight to West Huntspill, reaching ninety miles an hour as they crossed the Huntspill River.

They reached Pawlett in less than five minutes. PC Cole slowed on the approach to the village and forked right into Manor Road. A police car blocked the entrance to Manor Park on the right, but it pulled forward, allowing them through.

'Isn't this where the old nightclub was?' asked Dixon.

'Yes, Sir,' said Cole, 'the Manor. It had quite a reputation.'

'Before my time,' said Jane.

'And mine,' said Dixon.

'It closed in the late nineties, I think it was, and then this lot was built.'

Cole stopped the car and wound the window down to speak to a police officer who was standing on the pavement.

'I've got Inspector Dixon . . .'

'Park there and walk the rest of the way. Follow the road around to the left. Number 37 is in the far corner. Chief Inspector Bateman is Bronze Commander. He's in the house opposite.'

'Thanks.'

PC Cole turned round to speak to Dixon and Jane.

'It's all right, Constable, we heard,' said Dixon, taking off his seat belt.

They got out of the panda car. Dixon surveyed the scene. He counted five marked and two unmarked police cars along Manor Park. There was also a dog van and a black minibus with tinted windows. Two ambulances were waiting in the driveway of a house near the entrance to Manor Park and the helicopter was hovering over the fields at the back.

The houses themselves were detached, each standing on a good sized plot with a garage and large front and rear gardens. They were constructed of red brick and appeared, at least from the outside, to be of different designs. Some thought had clearly gone into the development of what seemed to be an affluent area.

Dixon and Jane walked along Manor Park to the bend. There was a cul-de-sac to the right containing the even numbered houses. He could see two more marked police cars blocking off the road to the left. Behind them crouched firearms officers, each pointing an automatic weapon at a house in the far corner. Dixon could see more armed officers in the upstairs windows of the houses opposite.

An officer met them on the bend opposite the junction. He was carrying an automatic weapon. He was dressed in black and wore a helmet and goggles.

'Detective Inspector Dixon?'

'Yes.'

'This way, Sir. And keep your head down.'

They ran along the front of the houses, crouching as low as they could, and turned down the side of the third house along. Once through the garden gate, the firearms officer stood up and opened the conservatory door for Dixon and Jane. They ran in to be greeted by WPC Louise Willmott.

'Hello, Sir. How are you feeling?'

'Terrible. But thank you for asking, Louise.'

'Painkillers and alcohol,' said Jane, 'not to mention a Tandoori last night.'

'I thought you were in hospital.'

'I was. And I'm beginning to wish I'd stayed there,' replied Dixon. 'Where's Mr Bateman?'

'Along the hall. The living room's on the left.'

'Thanks.'

Dixon walked through the kitchen and along the corridor towards the front of the house.

'Ah, you'll be Dixon?'

He turned to see an officer in full dress uniform standing in the doorway to the lounge. Dixon's face gave away what he was thinking.

'Don't ask. I was at a dinner in Taunton,' said Chief Inspector Bateman. 'I'm glad to see you're up and about.'

'Thank you, Sir.'

'Come in,' said Bateman, standing to one side to allow Dixon and Jane into the lounge.

'You'll be Constable Winter, no doubt?'

'Yes, Sir.'

'This is Inspector Watts, Firearms, and you know Sergeant Karen Marsden, family liaison, I think?'

'I do,' replied Dixon.

There were several other officers in the room who Chief Inspector Bateman did not introduce.

'Well, it's difficult to know with any degree of certainty what's gone on in there, to be frank,' he continued. 'All we know for sure is that they got home at about 11 p.m. The babysitter left shortly after that and then the neighbour heard a single gunshot just before midnight.'

'Is that it?' asked Dixon.

'Lots of shouting and screaming, of course.'

'And the house . . . ?'

'The property is registered in the name of one Thomas Woodman. He lives there with his daughter, Natalie, and her baby daughter. The son, Jonathan, is home on leave for his brother's funeral this coming Friday. We've spoken to Jonathan on the phone and all he would say is that he wants to speak to you. It's been quiet since then.'

'What about the son who died?'

'Is it relevant?' asked Bateman.

'Yes.'

'How do you . . . ?'

'I met the family in the Zalshah this evening or last night or whenever it was. Anyway, there is clearly a difference of opinion between father and son about how the brother died. Jonathan believes his brother was murdered. He was very drunk, though.'

Bateman turned to one of the officers sitting on the sofa.

'Find out who is investigating the death of the brother and get them here now, preferably with the file.'

'Yes, Sir,' replied the officer. 'What's the brother's name?'

'Noel,' replied Dixon. 'He died at a horse racing stables near Spaxton, so a Bridgwater officer will have it.'

'Thank you, Sir.'

The officer got up and left the room. Dixon sat down in the vacant seat on the sofa.

'I think I'd better sit down before I fall down.'

'Are you all right?' asked Bateman.

'Yes, Sir, thank you. It's just the painkillers, I think.'

'Get him a glass of water, someone,' said Bateman.

'What weapon does he have, do we know?' asked Dixon.

'No,' replied Watts. 'We've not got a look at it yet and he wouldn't be drawn on the phone. My guess would be a handgun of some sort.'

'Only, it'd be nice to know before I go in there.'

'You're not going in there,' said Bateman. 'And that's final. You can speak to him on the telephone.'

'Sir, with respect, he's asked to speak to me, almost certainly about the death of his brother, and it's not as if I pose much of a threat to him, is it?' Dixon raised his left arm and then immediately winced with the pain.

'No. We are not handing him another hostage on a plate. And that's an order.'

Karen Marsden handed Dixon a glass of water. He took a large swig. She then handed Dixon the telephone.

'Just hit the 'Redial' button, Sir. Jon will answer. He was quite agitated when we spoke to him at 2.30 a.m.'

'And you've not spoken to him since then?'

'No, Sir.'

'And there's been no movement in the house, either,' said Bateman.

Dixon pressed the 'Redial' button and waited.

'Is it on speakerphone?' asked Bateman.

'No, Sir, he'll be able to t . . .' Dixon stopped mid-sentence. He shook his head to silence those in the room.

'Who is this?'

'It's Nick Dixon, Jon. We met earlier.'

'You took your time.'

'How is everyone in there?'

'Fine.'

'They tell me you've got a gun . . .'

'Yes.'

'And you've used it?'

'Subtitles. I can't stand films with fucking subtitles.'

'Try changing the channel next time,' said Dixon.

'Nats had the gizmo.'

'I'm guessing you want to talk about your brother, Jon?'

'Yes.'

'What makes you think he was murdered?'

'Not on the phone.'

'Well, I can't come in, so you'll have to come out.'

Jon Woodman rang off.

'That went well,' said Bateman.

'It's a start, Sir,' said Dixon. 'If he doesn't ring me back, I'll try him again in five minutes.'

Dixon waited. Two minutes ticked by. Then the phone rang.

'Nick Dixon.'

'What's going on?'

'I'm waiting for the investigation file on Noel's death to arrive, Jon. Then I'm going to read it and we'll speak again.'

'Good.'

'Is everyone all right?'

'Yes.'

'Who have you got in there?'

'My father, Nats and the baby.'

'Let me speak to your father.'

'No.'

'Natalie then.'

'She's here.'

Dixon heard Jon speaking in the background. 'He wants to speak to you.'

Natalie came on the line.

'Hello?'

'Are you all right, Natalie?'

'Yes.'

'And your daughter?'

'Yes.'

'What's her name?'

'Leanne.'

'Where are you now?'

'We're on the sofa in the living room. Leanne's asleep.'

'And your father?'

'He's on the floor in the hall. Jon hit him wi—'

The phone was snatched from her grasp. Silence.

'Jon?'

Dixon waited.

'Look, Jon, my only concern is to get everyone out safely. Including you. Have you looked out of the window recently?'

'I can imagine.'

'Good. Now, what's happened to your father?'

'Fuck him. It's all his fault, anyway.'

'Is he dead, Jon?'

'No.'

'Is he conscious?'

'No.'

Karen Marsden passed Dixon a scribbled note.

'Hold on, Jon,' said Dixon. 'Someone's passing me a note. I'll have to put the phone down for a second.'

He placed the phone on his knee and read the note.

'The file will be here in two minutes. I'm going to read it and then call you back. In the meantime, you check on your father. OK?'

Silence.

'I need to know he's still breathing.'

'All right.'

Dixon rang off and turned to Chief Inspector Bateman.

'He's hit his father, I'm guessing with the gun, and left him unconscious on the floor in the hall. Natalie and the baby are on the sofa in the living room.'

'We need to get the father out,' said Bateman.

'We do,' replied Dixon. 'Any chance of a cup of tea?'

'I'll go,' said Jane.

———

Dixon was reading the file by the time Jane returned with a mug of tea. He turned first to the post mortem report prepared by Dr James Davidson at Musgrove Park Hospital. The report catalogued multiple injuries, all of them consistent with Noel having been kicked by a horse, including a fractured skull, eye socket, jaw and various ribs. The file also contained a bundle of photographs, which showed the imprint of a horseshoe or shoes on the body and a bite mark consistent with Noel having been bitten by a horse.

Next Dixon flicked through the witness statements. The owner of the stables, Georgina Harcourt, and the racehorse trainer, Michael Hesp, had been interviewed, along with the groom who had found Noel's body, Kevin Tanner. All confirmed that Noel had been found in Westbrook Warrior's stable at approximately 5.30 a.m., when Kevin Tanner had raised the alarm. He had been found lying in the back corner, behind Westbrook Warrior.

The horse was described as a three year old colt that was well known to be aggressive. Strict procedures had been adopted following a risk assessment conducted after a previous incident, and the standing instruction was that Westbrook Warrior was to be fed, watered and offered haylage over the stable door. No one was to go into the stable unless and until Westbrook Warrior had been tied up. Dixon noted Kevin Tanner's statement that Noel considered himself to have a special relationship with Westbrook Warrior. He had been known to go in the stable with the horse loose, according to Tanner.

The file had been marked 'Accidental Death', the coroner notified accordingly and the body released for cremation. An interim death certificate had also been issued pending the formal inquest.

'Well?' asked Bateman.

'Accidental death,' replied Dixon. 'Maybe Jon Woodman knows something we don't?'

'Ring him and ask him, then.'

'I intend to, Sir. I just need the loo first.'

'There's one under the stairs,' said Jane.

Dixon walked out of the lounge and along the hall to the downstairs lavatory. He switched the light on and closed the door without going in. Then he went into the kitchen and closed the kitchen door behind him.

'Give me your tabard, Louise.'

'But . . .'

'Just do it. Please.'

Louise Willmott took off her fluorescent tabard and helped Dixon put it on.

——— ———

'Oh, for fuck's sake,' said Inspector Watts.

'What is it?' asked Bateman, spinning round to see Watts looking across the road through a gap in the curtains.

'You'd better come and have a look, Sir.'

Chief Inspector Bateman looked out of the front window. He could see Dixon standing on the doorstep of number 37.

'Stand down,' said Watts, into his radio.

'I hope he knows what he's doing,' said Bateman.

Jane ran forward and looked out of the window, just in time to see the door open and Dixon go in.

She took a deep breath and then looked at Bateman.

'He does, Sir,' she said.

——— ———

Dixon took two steps into the hall before he heard the front door close behind him. He turned to face Jon Woodman. He was holding a handgun in his right hand.

'An old 9 mm Browning,' said Dixon. 'I fired one of those on Salisbury Plain once, with the cadets.'

'What the f . . . ?'

'Where's your father?'

'I dragged him into the kitchen.'

'OK, here's what's going to happen. I'm going to check on him now, and then I'm going to get two officers in here to get him out. Then we'll talk.'

'I say what's going to happen now. Not you. I'm in charge.'

'Oh, really?' replied Dixon. 'What makes you think that?'

'I've got the fucking gun.'

'And I've got twenty more outside. Machine guns too.'

Jon Woodman shook his head. Dixon continued.

'So, we'll do this my way or not at all. Then everybody might get out of here in one piece. OK?'

Jon raised the gun and pointed it at Dixon's forehead.

'Think about it, Jon. You're facing firearms offences at the moment, assuming your father lives and neither he nor Natalie press charges. I'm guessing you want me to look into Noel's death, which I'm happy to do. But we all need to walk out of here for that.'

Jon hesitated before lowering the gun.

'What do you want me to do?'

'Wait here while I check your father.'

Dixon walked through into the kitchen. Tom Woodman was lying face down on the floor in front of the sink. Dixon checked his neck for a pulse. He was still alive.

'I'm going to arrange for two officers to come in and get him out, Jon. You wait in the lounge. And for heaven's sake, stay out of sight.'

Dixon reached into his pocket for his mobile phone and rang Jane.

'Nick, are you all right?'

'Yes, fine. Put it on speakerphone and then pass me to Bateman, will you?'

Jane selected loudspeaker and then passed the phone to Chief Inspector Bateman.

'What the bloody hell do you thi—?'

'Do you mind if we talk about that later, Sir? I've got him to agree to let his father out. I'll need a stretcher and two officers to come in and get him.'

'Two of my lads can go in, Sir,' said Watts.

'Where will you be?' asked Bateman.

'We'll be in the living room, with the door closed,' replied Dixon.

'We could . . .'

Dixon cut Watts off in mid-sentence.

'There's no need to try anything. I'm quite confident I can bring him out, Sir. We just need to get his father to a hospital as soon as we can.'

'OK. Give me a minute.'

'Ring me back when you're ready to come in,' said Dixon.

Dixon went into the lounge and sat on the sofa next to Natalie. Jon Woodman was pacing up and down in front of the fireplace. Dixon noticed a single bullet hole in the middle of the television screen.

'Who do you think you are? Elvis Presley?' asked Dixon. He thought he saw Jon Woodman smile.

'What's happening?' asked Natalie.

'They're sending someone in to collect your father and then we're going to have a chat about Noel's death. Aren't we, Jon?'

'Yes.'

Dixon's phone rang.

'Yes, Sir.'

'We're ready to come in and get the father,' said Bateman.

'I'm putting you on speakerphone, Sir, so Jon can hear what's going to happen for himself.'

'Fine. We have two unarmed officers ready with a stretcher.'

'Good,' said Dixon. 'I'll unlock the front door. Tell them to wait thirty seconds and then come in. I'll be back in the lounge by then. He's in the kitchen, which is straight through to the back of the house.'

'OK.'

'I'll keep you on the line, Sir. Are you happy with that, Jon?'

'Yes.'

Dixon went into the hall and unlocked the front door. He then returned to the lounge, closing the door behind him. They listened to footsteps approaching along the front path and then the front door opening. After a short pause, the footsteps continued along the hall to the kitchen. They could hear muffled voices.

'You take his feet.'

And then the sound of footsteps moving back along the hall and the front door closing again.

'We've got him,' said Bateman.

'Thank you, Sir. I'm going to lock the front door again now. I'd be grateful to know how he is as soon as there's any news.'

'Will do.'

Dixon rang off and then locked the front door.

'How about a cup of tea after all that excitement?'

'Let's cut to the chase then, Jon. Two questions interest me. Firstly, why did you say it was all your father's fault and, secondly, why do you think Noel was murdered?' asked Dixon.

'My father hated Noel. He hated his own son. The bastard threw him out when he was seventeen, sevenfuckingteen, and left him to fend for himself.'

'Why?'

'Noel was gay,' said Natalie.

'He threw him out with no money, nothing!' screamed Jon.

'Just because he was gay?'

'Yes.'

'What did your mother say?'

'She's dead.'

'What did Noel do?'

'Do you want me to spell it out?'

'Yes,' replied Dixon. 'I find it avoids any misunderstandings.'

Jon Woodman turned away.

'He was a rent boy,' said Natalie. 'It was the only way he could make any money.'

'Until he found horses. He loved horses,' said Jon.

'Then he got the job at the racing stables,' said Natalie. 'He was going to be a jockey.'

'OK, so why do you think he was murdered?'

'The last time we spoke, he said he knew something and was going to go public with it,' said Jon.

'Did he say what it was?'

'No. Just that it was big and he was gonna blow the whistle on it.'

Dixon turned to Natalie.

'Did he say anything to you?'

'No.'

'Is that it?' asked Dixon.

'What do you mean, "is that it"?' screamed Jon. 'Isn't that enough?'

'Probably not, no. The post mortem report details multiple injuries consistent with being kicked by a horse, there are horseshoe marks on his body and he was found in a stable with an aggressive colt. A horse he knew he shouldn't have gone in with, apparently.'

Dixon's phone bleeped, announcing the arrival of a text message.

DCI Lewis is here. Jx

'What's that?' asked Jon.

'My boss is here,' replied Dixon.

'So, what happens now?' asked Jon. 'I'm not going out there until someone does something. And neither are you.'

'We're going to need more than just one conversation about blowing the whistle on something big to get a murder investigation authorised, Jon.'

'He was murdered. I know he was murdered,' said Jon.

'I'll make a deal with you, then,' said Dixon, standing up. Jon backed away, still pointing the gun at Dixon.

'What?'

'You're going to have to trust me. I'm assuming you do; otherwise I wouldn't be here.'

'Yes.'

'Good. Do you remember the chap I was sitting with at the Zalshah last night?'

'Sort of.'

'His name's Roger Poland. He's the senior forensic pathologist at Musgrove Park.'

'So what?'

'Natalie, do you consent to a second post mortem on Noel?'

'Why me?'

'Your father is unconscious and Jon is . . . indisposed, shall we say? That makes you the next of kin.'

'What good would it do?' she asked.

'Well, that's the deal, isn't it?' replied Dixon. 'A second post mortem on Noel by Roger Poland. He's good, very good. And if he thinks Noel was murdered, that will be enough to trigger a formal murder investigation.'

'And if he doesn't?' asked Jon.

'Then Noel wasn't murdered. And you'll just have to accept that. Either way, you put down the gun and come out.'

'What will happen to me?'

'You'll be arrested and remanded in custody. Then you'll go to Exeter Prison. But that's better than the alternative, believe me.'

'I suppose.'

'We can get the second post mortem done this morning. I can pay a visit to the racing yard at the same time.'

'You're not going anywhere.'

'I need to go out there and set this up, for starters, Jon.'

'No.'

'I'll keep in touch by phone and I'll be back, too. One way or the other.'

Silence.

'Do you want someone else to investigate it?'

'No.'

'Then you have to let me out.'

Dixon stared at Jon Woodman. Beads of sweat appeared on Jon's forehead. He began to tremble.

'It's crunch time, Jon.'

Silence.

'I'm offering you what you want. But we need to get it done today. He's being cremated on Friday, don't forget.'

'OK, OK,' replied Jon. 'But you're coming back?'

'I am. And when I do, good news or bad, you're putting that bloody thing down and coming out. Agreed?'

'Agreed.'

'Where is Noel?'

'He's at the Co-op in Bridgwater,' said Natalie.

Dixon took his phone out of his pocket and rang Jane.

'What's happening?'

'I'm coming out in two minutes. Tell Watts to make sure I don't get shot, will you?'

'Leave it with me.'

Dixon turned back to Natalie and Jon.

'No one will come in before I get back, so stay out of sight and don't do anything stupid.'

Dixon walked out into the hall and closed the lounge door behind him. He unlocked the front door and then rang Jane again.

'I'm coming out now. Ready?'

'All set,' replied Jane.

Dixon opened the door and stepped out into the light from the arc lamps. He held his right hand up and then walked slowly forwards along the path. Jane came out to meet him.

'You all right?'

'Fine.'

'Lewis is hopping mad.'

'He'll get over it.'

'What's the story then, Dixon?' asked Bateman. 'We can come back to the flagrant breach of a direct order later.'

'I've agreed with Jon that Roger Poland will do a second post mortem on Noel this morning. Natalie has given her consent as next of kin. While Roger's doing that, Jane and I will visit the racing yard and see what we can find.'

'And the point of all this?'

'Well, for a start, once it's done, Jon will come out. If he's right, we'll also find evidence of a murder.'

'Great. So, we just wait a few hours and then tell him Poland found nothing,' said Watts.

'He's going to be pointing a 9 mm Browning pistol at me when I tell him it's been done so if you think I'm going to try to blag him, you're . . .'

'What Inspector Dixon means is that it needs to be done, and done properly, if we are to bring this situation to an end satisfactorily,' said DCI Lewis.

'Thank you, Sir.'

'Well, let's get on with it then,' said Bateman. 'And keep us posted.'

⌣

'Would you mind explaining what the bloody hell's going on?' asked Lewis as they walked out through the conservatory. 'You're supposed to be safely tucked up in hospital and the next thing I know I'm getting a call at 4 a.m. to tell me you've just wandered into an armed siege.'

'I discharged myself from hospital, Sir.'

'You're supposed to be off sick.'

'I'm fine,' replied Dixon.

'So, we've got a gunman who thinks his brother's been murdered?'

'That's the bones of it, yes.'

'Where's the body?'

'The Co-op in Bridgwater.'

'Well, you can wake Roger Poland up. I'll get onto the Co-op and get the body moved back to Musgrove Park.'

'Thank you, Sir.'

'I really should be splitting you two up now.'

'These are exceptional circumstances, surely?' asked Dixon.

'We'll run with that for the time being. But I'm relying on you to keep him out of trouble, Jane.'

'Yes, Sir.'

Chapter Two

It was just before 6 a.m. when PC Cole dropped Dixon and Jane back at the cottage in Brent Knoll. Jane took a shower and changed clothes while Dixon rang Roger Poland.

'Hello?'

'Morning, Roger. It's Nick.'

'What time is it?'

'Six o'clock.'

'What the . . . ?'

'It's a long story but I need you to do a PM as soon as you can. Today. Now.'

'Now?'

'You remember last night—the soldier who thought his brother had been killed?'

'Yes.'

'He's holed up in a house in Pawlett. He's got a gun and won't come out until we've looked into his brother's death.'

'We?'

'Yes, we.'

'I've got a meeting at 10 a.m.'

'Cancel it.'

'You owe me one for this.'

'I do. The body's at the Co-op at the moment. DCI Lewis is arranging for it to be moved back to Musgrove Park as we speak.'

'OK. I'll get over there now and read Davidson's notes. Are you coming over?'

'We're going to the stables first. Then we'll come on to you. Ring me if you find anything.'

'Will do.'

Dixon rang off and then picked up the file. He turned to the witness statement from Georgina Harcourt.

'I am the proprietor of Gidley's Racing Stables . . .'

He opened his laptop and searched Google for 'Gidley's Racing Spaxton'. The first result came from michaelhespracing.co.uk. Dixon read the meta description out loud.

'Michael Hesp Racing is based at Gidley's Racing Stables, Spaxton, Somerset. Michael trains National Hunt and Flat horses on the edge of the Quantocks in Somerset . . .'

Dixon clicked on the link and looked at each page of the website. About Us, Gallery, Horses, Ownership and Results. He was just finishing when Jane appeared with two mugs of coffee. She was about to speak when his phone rang.

'Nick Dixon.'

'It's Karen Marsden, Sir. Just to say that Tom Woodman is conscious and he's going to be all right.'

'Thanks, Karen. I'll let Jon know.'

Dixon rang off and then dialled Jon Woodman.

'Jon? It's Nick Dixon.'

'What's happening?'

'Noel's body is on the way back to Musgrove Park now and Roger Poland will be doing a second post mortem, as agreed. I'm going to Spaxton and then on to the hospital.'

'Good.'

'Your father's going to be fine. He's awake now and is going to be OK.'

'Fuck him.'

Jon Woodman rang off.

Dixon turned to Jane. 'You can choose your friends . . .'

'Quite.'

A long gravel drive led to a small visitors' car park on the right just before they reached Gidley's Racing Stables. It was just after 8 a.m. when Dixon and Jane arrived in his beaten up old Land Rover. Jane had driven and Dixon had spent most of the journey on the phone. Noel Woodman's body had arrived at Musgrove Park Hospital and Roger Poland had made a start on the second post mortem. He had also recovered all of the samples taken from the first post mortem, conducted by James Davidson.

Dixon had telephoned Jon Woodman to keep him up to date with developments and rang off just as Jane was parking the car. He could see two horse lorries, one large and one small, parked off to the left. They walked into a courtyard formed by the old farmhouse on the left, red brick stable blocks on each side and an open fronted hay barn and feed store opposite the house. Dixon could see the roof of a larger barn behind the stables. He counted five stables on each side with a concrete plinth along the front of both blocks. The courtyard itself was block paved and sloped towards a drain in the centre.

Two horses were tied up outside their stables, eating hay from nets. All of the other horses were standing with their heads over their stable doors. All except one. The top half of the door was open but blocked off by heavy steel bars. The name on the door told Dixon he need look no further for Westbrook Warrior's stable.

He was watching the horses tearing hay from their nets when Jane tapped him on the arm and nodded towards the farmhouse. They were being watched from a ground floor window. A groom appeared from an alleyway between the stables and the barn in the far right corner of the yard. He was pushing a wheelbarrow and turned along the front of the block, heading towards the open stables. Dixon shouted over to him.

'Excuse me?'

No response.

'He's wearing earphones,' said Jane.

'They're a bloody nuisance, those things.'

Dixon tried again. Louder this time.

'Oi.'

The groom stopped and looked over. He took the earphones out of his ears.

'Yes.'

'We're looking for Michael Hesp.'

'He'll be in the house.'

'Get him, will you,' said Dixon.

'Who are you?'

'Police.'

'Oh, right.'

Dixon turned to Jane.

'You wait. A Barbour jacket and green wellies.'

'Tweed,' said Jane.

They heard the farmhouse door slam.

'Bad luck, Jane,' said Dixon.

'How could you possibly have known that?'

'Call it an educated guess. It'll be tweed on race days.'

'Can I help you?' asked Hesp.

'Yes. I am Detective Inspector Dixon and this is Detective Constable Winter. We're investigating the death of Noel Woodman.'

'I thought that was closed. Accidental death, surely?'

'Something happened to open it again, Sir,' said Dixon.

'Can I ask what?'

'I can't say, I'm afraid.'

Dixon spotted Hesp's nervous glance in the direction of the farmhouse.

'Well, how can I help?'

'Can you show us the static caravan where he was living, please?'

'Yes, of course, follow me.'

Dixon and Jane followed Michael Hesp across the yard and into the alleyway between the barn and the corner of the stable block. At the end they walked straight on. To his right, Dixon could see a muddy path leading to the muckheap. To his left was a large American barn. The doors were open and he counted ten more stables inside. They walked along the side of the barn and turned left. The static caravan was hidden from view behind it.

'It's sheltered from the prevailing wind and out of sight,' said Hesp.

They heard footsteps inside the caravan.

'It's occupied?' asked Dixon.

'Life goes on, Inspector. And we had to replace Noel.'

'Where are his belongings? Have the family collected them?'

'Not yet. They're boxed up and in the barn over there.'

'How many boxes are there?'

'Two.'

'We'll get them in the back of the Land Rover before we go.'

'Fine,' replied Hesp.

'Let's have a look at Westbrook Warrior then,' said Dixon.

'Follow me.'

They walked back round into the yard and along the front of the stable block. Hesp stopped outside Westbrook Warrior's stable.

'Can we get him out?' asked Dixon.

'Er, yes, I suppose so. Kevin, can you come and give me a hand, please?'

Dixon and Jane stood back and watched while Kevin Tanner opened the stable door just wide enough to slide in. He approached the Warrior at the shoulder, making no sudden movements and avoiding eye contact. Then he reached up and put a headcollar on him. Hesp opened the door and Tanner led the horse out into the yard.

'Stand clear,' said Hesp. 'He kicks.'

Westbrook Warrior was jet black with a white blaze and four white socks. Dixon estimated he was nearly seventeen hands.

'He's a big lad.'

'Seventeen two,' said Tanner. 'He flies the hurdles.'

'He's not shod?' asked Dixon.

'We took his plates off after what happened to Noel,' replied Hesp. 'And he's not racing again for a week or so.'

'Where are the shoes now?' asked Dixon.

'No idea. The farrier would've taken them.'

'Who is he?'

'Simon Whitfield. He comes over from Wellington.'

Dixon walked around the front of Westbrook Warrior, looking at his hooves. He took out his iPhone and took a photograph of each hoof.

'Can we pick up his back feet?' he asked.

'Must we?'

'If you can.'

Kevin Tanner tied Westbrook Warrior to his hay net and then picked up a front leg. At the same time, Hesp picked up a back foot. Dixon moved in and took a photograph of the underside of the hoof. They then repeated the process for the other hoof.

'If he's off balance, he can't kick,' said Hesp, letting go of the back leg and stepping back.

'Who's his owner?' asked Dixon.

'He's owned by a syndicate. Most of our horses are these days, although we have some that aren't. Georgina can give you the names and addresses.'

'Is that Mrs Harcourt watching from the window?' asked Dixon.

The question caught Hesp off guard. He spun round and looked up at the farmhouse. The figure in the window stepped back into the shadows.

'Er, yes.'

'Perhaps later, then. I'll just have the farrier's number for now, if you've got it handy.'

Hesp took out his mobile phone and read off Simon Whitfield's number. Jane wrote it in her notebook.

'The straw from the stable will be on the muckheap, I suppose?'

'Yes.'

'What does he eat, apart from hay?'

'It's haylage actually. His hard feed is Dodson & Horrell Race-horse Cubes.'

'What about the others?'

'Some are on the cubes, others on mix. We've got a couple on pure oats too. It varies.'

'How many horses have you got here?'

'Sixteen at the moment.'

'One last question. For now.'

'Fire away,' said Hesp.

'Forgive me if it sounds rude but your results . . . they're not good, are they?'

'We've had some bad luck. And a bad run. It'll turn around.'

'I'm right, though. They're not good?'

'No, they're not.'

'Thank you.'

They loaded the boxes of Noel's belongings into the back of the Land Rover and drove slowly down the drive. Dixon rang the farrier.

'Simon Whitfield.'

'My name is Detective Inspector Dixon. I'm investigating the death of Noel Woodman. I understand you're Westbrook Warrior's farrier.'

'Yes, I am.'

'We need to speak to you now, Mr Whitfield. Where are you?'

'I'm on a job.'

'Where?'

'On a farm near Wellington.'

Dixon wrote down the address.

'How much longer will you be there?'

'About an hour.'

'We're on our way. Please make sure you don't leave until we get there.'

They arrived at West Town Farm on the outskirts of Wellington just before 9.30 a.m. Simon Whitfield was waiting by his van, drinking coffee from a plastic Thermos flask cup.

'Thank you for waiting, Mr Whitfield.'

'No problem. How can I help?'

'We need to have a chat with you about Westbrook Warrior's shoes.'

'Plates. They're called racing plates.'

'Thanks,' replied Dixon. 'Is he usually shod, or only when he's racing?'

'Michael keeps them shod. Some trainers don't, but he does.'

'When did you last shoe Westbrook Warrior, then?'

'The day before the accident. He was racing the next day at Taunton.'

'Mr Hesp told me you took the shoes . . . plates . . . off after the accident?'

'Yes, on the Monday.'

'Why was that?'

'He said he wanted them off for safety reasons.'

Jane was taking notes. Simon Whitfield finished his coffee and threw the dregs on the ground. Dixon continued.

'Where are the plates now?'

'They were new, so I put 'em on another horse. Waste not, want not and all that.'

'Which horse?'

'No idea. Could've been any one of a number, I'm afraid.'

'Is there any way you can find out?'

'Not really. I'd have reshaped them and they'd have gone in the forge first too, don't forget.'

'Is there anything unusual about Warrior's hooves?'

'They're cut a bit squarer than normal, I suppose, but he's got a good solid hoof, to be honest.'

'Size?'

'Average, for a thoroughbred.'

'Show me one of these racing plates, then?'

'Sure.'

They walked around to the back of Whitfield's van. He opened the doors to reveal his portable gas forge, which looked like a large black microwave oven, and various wooden boxes containing shoes and nails. He reached into a box and produced a new horseshoe. He handed it to Dixon.

'This is a normal horseshoe. I buy them in boxes of ten pairs. Cheap as chips. I heat them in the forge and then shape them to the horse's hoof, once I've trimmed it, of course.'

Dixon looked at the shoe. It was the perfect horseshoe shape, dark grey and heavier than he had expected. There were five nail holes either side. On the underside was a deep groove.

'How much are they?'

'You can get five pairs for two quid.'

'And they come in different sizes?'

'Yes, that's a five inch.'

'Is this one front or back, or are they the same?'

'No, that's a front shoe. The hinds, we call them, are a slightly different shape.' He reached into the box and then handed Dixon another shoe.

'That's a hind. See the shape? It's got slightly straighter sides.'

'Can we keep these?' said Dixon, handing the shoes to Jane.

'Yeah, sure.'

'But this isn't what Westbrook Warrior had on?'

'Fuck, no,' replied Whitfield.

He went around to the side door of the van, opened it, and took out a plastic box.

'This is a Victory EC Queens aluminium racing plate with toe clip.' He handed two shoes to Dixon. 'This one's the front and this one the hind, with two clips. This ridge is called a toe grab. It's for extra grip.'

'And these are what he'd have been wearing when he kicked Noel?'

'Yes.'

'Same size?'

'Yep.'

The differences were obvious. It was thinner, narrower and lighter. It also had seven nail holes on each side, instead of five, and a distinct ridge underneath.

'Can we keep these?'

'They're a bit more expensive . . .'

'You'll get them back.'

'Yeah, that's fine then.'

'What about the nails?' asked Jane.

'They're different too,' replied Whitfield. 'Here, have a couple of each.'

'And Westbrook Warrior himself, he's aggressive, I'm told?' asked Dixon.

'He is. Call it an occupational hazard.'

'Thank you, Mr Whitfield. You've been most helpful.'

'What's the matter?'

'I forgot my Tramadol,' said Dixon, shifting uncomfortably in the passenger seat of the Land Rover.

'Where are they?'

'In the kitchen.'

'You idiot.'

'Sympathy and understanding. Just what I need.'

'We'll find a chemist in Wellington. It's on the way.'

Jane drove along Fore Street and parked on the double yellow lines outside Superdrug. Dixon was deep in thought, and yet alert enough to notice the traffic warden making a beeline for his car. He waved her over, produced his warrant card and then watched in the wing mirror as she went in search of another victim.

'Was that a traffic warden?' asked Jane.

'Yes, but she's gone. You're all right.'

'Me?'

'You're driving.'

Jane's reply was lost in the noise of the old diesel engine starting up. She reached over and dropped a plastic bag into Dixon's lap. It contained a bacon and egg sandwich, a bottle of water and a box of Solpadeine Max.

'Breakfast, too. You, Jane, are a bloody marvel.'

He reached into his inside jacket pocket and took out his insulin pen. Despite the sling, he was able to hold the end of the pen in his left hand and turn the dial to the correct number of units with his right. He then pushed the needle into his right thigh through his trousers and pressed the button with his thumb.

'I'm not sure I'd ever get used to that,' said Jane.

'There's not a lot of choice.'

'I suppose.'

'Right, let's get over to Musgrove Park and don't spare the . . .'

'Don't say it.'

The second post mortem was well under way by the time Dixon and Jane arrived at Musgrove Park Hospital. They watched Roger Poland at work from the comparative safety of the anteroom until one of the laboratory assistants spotted them and alerted Poland. He waved at them to go in.

'Tracey, a mask for the inspector, please,' said Poland.

'No, I'm fine, really.'

Noel Woodman was lying on the slab. He had short dark hair, although most of it had been shaved off, and the top of his skull had been removed and then replaced. Rudimentary stitches held it in place. He had extensive facial injuries that the funeral director had attempted to hide with make up. Decomposition was not well advanced, which Dixon took to be evidence of the effectiveness of the available cold storage facilities. Noel's chest cavity was open, which turned both Dixon's and Jane's stomachs.

'I'm onto internal injuries,' explained Poland. 'There are several broken ribs and a right sided pulmonary laceration where the rib has penetrated the lung.'

'He's small, isn't he?' said Jane.

'Well, he was going to be a jockey, don't forget,' replied Dixon.

'Ideal size for that, I'd have thought,' said Poland.

'Are these the samples?' asked Dixon, looking at a collection of small jars on the metal worktop at the foot of the slab.

'Yes. Davidson was very thorough. We've got blood and tissue samples, stomach contents, the usual stuff, and also two lots of horse dung, one from his nose and the other from his mouth.'

'Anything interesting?'

'No drink or drugs or anything like that, but I haven't run those tests again. Do you want me to?'

'No,' replied Dixon, 'not at this stage.'

Dixon walked around to the top of the slab and looked at Noel's head injuries.

'What about the cause of death, then?'

'Davidson got that right too, I'm pleased to say. Multiple injuries. Any number of which would have killed him on their own. He had the severe pulmonary laceration, of course. Very severe sharp impact head injuries, which penetrated the skull. An epidural haematoma. Massive internal bleeding. Need I go on?'

'No. I get the picture,' replied Dixon. 'What about the cause of those injuries, then?'

'That's easy,' replied Poland. 'We'll start with this bundle of photos.' He pointed to a photograph of the left side of Noel's forehead.

'What do you see?'

'The imprint of a horseshoe,' replied Jane.

'Exactly,' said Poland. 'Tracey, wash the make up off his face, will you?'

'Where are the others on the body?' asked Dixon.

'Two on the back of his head, a partial one on his jaw and others on his back and chest. That one broke the ribs.'

'Do we have a diagram of them?'

'I can do one, easily,' said Poland.

'Yes, please.'

Dixon and Jane waited while Poland marked the horseshoe imprints on two outline drawings of a human body, one marked 'front' and the other 'back'.

'I'm assuming we can't read anything into the orientation of the marks without knowing Noel's relative position to the horse?' asked Dixon.

'And whether Westbrook Warrior kicked him with his front or his back hooves,' said Jane.

'That's right,' replied Poland. 'My understanding is that an aggressive horse will attack with its front hooves and teeth, and we do have the bite mark as well, of course.'

'But if Noel was behind him, he'd kick with his back legs?' asked Dixon.

'He would.'

'Which is the clearest imprint?'

'The one on his forehead. The partial on his jaw is clearish too. Why?'

'Can we see it?'

'Yes, of course.'

Poland opened the album again and turned to the last of the photographs. 'This is it,' he said, handing the album to Dixon. 'Here, come and have a look.'

The laboratory assistant, Tracey, had finished cleaning the make up off Noel's face. Dixon leaned over and stared at the imprint on his forehead.

'Are all the imprints from the same shoe?' he asked, without looking up.

'As far as we can tell, the same type of shoe, yes. Some are blurred due to his clothing, of course, but the force was such that there's still a clear mark.'

'But there's the imprint of more than one shoe?'

'I'd need to check that. Davidson certainly didn't look at it.'

Dixon turned to Jane. 'Open your handbag a second, will you, Jane?'

Dixon reached into it and took out a horseshoe. He handed it to Poland.

'Like this?'

'Yes, that's it. You've got the deep groove and you can count the five nails either side.'

'And this is definitely the same type of shoe that killed him?'

'Yes. Why?'

'Because these are bog standard horseshoes. Twenty pence each, for heaven's sake. And very heavy. It'd be like a sprinter running in diving boots.'

Dixon took a racing plate from Jane's handbag and handed it to Poland.

'This is an aluminium racing plate and this is what Westbrook Warrior was wearing at the time. The farrier put four new ones on him the day before, ready for the race at Taunton.'

Poland looked at the racing plate. 'Seven nail holes.'

'Exactly.'

Poland looked again at the photographs. Then at the racing plate.

'There's a ridge at the front here, presumably for extra grip. That's not imprinted on the body, either.'

'So, Westbrook Warrior didn't kick him?' asked Jane.

'No, he didn't,' replied Poland, 'which gives us an unexplained death, doesn't it?'

'Bollocks,' said Dixon. 'He was murdered and thrown into the stable to make it look like the horse kicked him to death.'

'That's certainly one interpretation of it, yes,' said Poland.

'What are the others?' asked Dixon.

'Well . . .'

Dixon continued. 'Let me ask you this, then. Bearing in mind his injuries, is it possible he got in that stable under his own steam before he lay down and died?'

'No, definitely not,' replied Poland.

'So, a person or persons unknown killed him somewhere else and then . . .' Dixon's voice tailed off. 'Pass me the photos.'

He stared at the photograph of the imprint on Noel's forehead.

'Jane, pass me the nails, will you?'

He put the photo album down on the worktop and stood looking at it with the nails in the palm of his right hand.

Dixon nodded. 'That's it.' He passed the album to Poland. 'What shape are the nail heads, Roger?'

Poland looked at the photograph. 'Round.'

'Hold out your hand.'

Dixon dropped the nails into the palm of Poland's hand.

'They're square.'

'They are,' replied Dixon. 'We need to know how many shoes are imprinted on his body, Roger. Can you do that?'

'Yes.'

'Perhaps produce a 3D image of them from the imprints?'

'Yes, why?'

'Because if I'm right, we'll find that all of the injuries were caused by one shoe.'

'One shoe?' asked Jane.

'Yes, I don't think he was kicked by a horse at all. I think he was hit by a piece of wood with a horseshoe nailed to it, to make it look like he was kicked by a horse. What do you think?'

'It's certainly possible,' said Poland.

'Either that or he was kicked to death by a one legged horse.'

Poland turned to Jane. 'He has such a way with words.'

'He was then thrown into the stable. I'm guessing now, but I suspect that Westbrook Warrior was taken by surprise, spun round and bit him.'

'We need to get the scenes of crime team over there as soon as possible,' said Jane.

'Looks like I've got my work cut out too,' said Poland.

'At least you know what to look for now. Will you be able to tell if the bite mark was made post mortem?'

'Leave it with me.'

'We've still got to get Jon Woodman out of that house, don't forget,' said Jane.

'Yes. C'mon, let's get over there now. Thanks, Roger. I owe you one.'

'You do.'

The police car pulled forward to allow Jane to turn into Manor Park just before midday. Dixon had rung ahead to tell both Chief Inspector Bateman and Jon Woodman that he was on his way. He had also asked DCI Lewis to meet them there and could see his car parked in the driveway of a vacant house.

Dixon and Jane were met on the bend by an armed officer, as before, and escorted along the front of the houses to the makeshift incident room in the house opposite number 37. This time Dixon made no effort to 'stay low' as the firearms officer had suggested.

He was walking into the conservatory when his phone rang.

'Nick, it's Roger. It's the same shoe.'

'How can you tell?'

'One of the nails has a defect in the rim. You can see it as plain as day in each of the imprints on his head. If you're looking for it, of course.'

'What about the others on his body?'

'They're not as clear due to his clothing. But the head injuries were the immediately fatal ones and it's the same shoe every time. No doubt about it.'

'Thanks, Roger.'

'It's a bit embarrassing Davidson missed it, but I have some sympathy for him. It must have seemed a straightforward accidental death.'

'There's a police officer who's going to be just as embarrassed, I can assure you.'

'And rightly so,' said Poland.

'But you'd agree Noel was murdered?'

'It looks like it. I've got a bit more work to do but, yes, I'd say he was murdered.'

'Look for anything to suggest he was killed elsewhere and where that might have been, will you?'

'Will do.'

'And thanks again, Roger.'

'Well, Dixon, what have you got?' asked Bateman.

'Noel Woodman was murdered, Sir.'

'Go on.'

'We start with Jon's statement that Noel was about to blow the whistle on something big. Noel's then found dead in Westbrook Warrior's stable, apparently kicked to death.'

'Yes.'

'According to Roger Poland, this is an exact match for the horseshoe that inflicted the fatal injuries.'

Dixon handed the standard shoe to Bateman, who looked at it and then passed it to DCI Lewis.

'And this is an exact match for the shoes Westbrook Warrior was wearing at the time. This is an aluminium racing plate. The differences are obvious.'

Bateman examined the racing plate.

'They are,' he said.

'Therefore,' continued Dixon, 'Westbrook Warrior did not kick Noel Woodman.'

'Agreed.'

'Pass me the file, Jane.'

Dixon took out the bundle of photographs and turned to the photo of Noel's forehead.

'What do you notice about the nails?'

Bateman looked at the photograph and then passed it to Lewis.

'They're round headed,' said Lewis.

'That's right, Sir. Carpentry nails. These are horseshoe nails,' said Dixon, holding a nail up in front of Bateman and Lewis.

'Square headed?' asked Bateman.

'That's right. So, here's what I think happened. Someone who doesn't know the difference between a standard horseshoe and a racing plate nailed a shoe to a piece of wood . . .'

'Using the wrong nails,' said Lewis.

'Yes, Sir. And then beat his brains out with it. Literally. All of the fatal injuries were inflicted by the same shoe. He or she then threw the body into Westbrook Warrior's stable to make it look as though he'd been kicked.'

'And the bite mark?' asked Lewis.

'I'm guessing now, but I expect that was inflicted by the horse, probably post mortem. Poland is looking at that now.'

'Wouldn't it need two people to pick up a body and throw it?' asked Bateman.

'Depends on the people, Sir,' replied Dixon, 'but Noel was going to be a jockey, don't forget.'

'He's very small, Sir,' said Jane.

'And Poland will confirm this?' asked Lewis.

'He will.'

'Who the bloody hell was in charge of this investigation?' asked Bateman.

Dixon looked at the front of the file.

'DS Unwin, Sir.'

'And I don't think much of the first post mortem, either.'

'We'd better get the Scientific lot over to Spaxton immediately,' said Lewis. 'I'll deal with that, Nick. You need to get over the road and get them out of that house. I'll get onto the coroner too.'

'A murder investigation it is, then?' asked Bateman.

'Yes,' replied Lewis.

'Who's going to run that with Dixon off sick?' asked Bateman. 'You're a bit thin on the ground in CID at the moment.'

Dixon glared at DCI Lewis.

'Do you feel up to it, Nick?'

'Yes.'

'That's settled, then,' said Lewis.

———

Dixon rang Jon Woodman.

'I'm coming over, Jon.'

'Good.'

'Everyone OK?'

'Yes.'

'All right, I'm on my way now.'

Dixon put on a fluorescent tabard and walked across the road to number 37. Once inside, he sat on the sofa next to Natalie and Leanne.

'You both OK?'

'Yes, fine. Bored, though. Can't even watch the telly.'

'Well?' asked Jon.

'It looks like you were right. Noel was murdered.'

'I knew it. I fucking knew it!'

'A murder investigation has been authorised and the scientific services team are on their way to Spaxton now.'

'And?'

Dixon produced the horseshoes from his coat pocket.

'This is the type of shoe that killed Noel. This one is what Westbrook Warrior was wearing at the time. So, it couldn't have been him.'

'How was that missed?'

'They weren't looking for it. It seemed like a straightforward accident,' replied Dixon.

'Useless gits.'

'It looks like a shoe was nailed to a piece of wood or something to make it look like he was kicked.'

'So what happens now?'

'Well, I'm in charge of the investigation so I need to get back out there. We had a deal, remember, so I'm expecting you to come too.'

Jon looked at his feet and then at the gun in his right hand. He released the magazine, letting it drop to the floor, and then, holding the gun by the barrel, handed it to Dixon. Dixon checked the chamber was empty and the safety catch was on.

'You'll let me know what happens?' said Jon.

'Of course I will.'

Dixon rang Jane.

'I've got the gun. We're coming out. Natalie and the baby first, then Jon, then me. OK?'

'Got it.'

Dixon rang off.

'When we get out there, Jon, lie down on the lawn with your hands . . .'

'I know the drill.'

'OK.'

Dixon opened the front door. Natalie and Leanne went out first. Natalie ran across the lawn, with Leanne in her arms, towards Karen Marsden, the family liaison officer. Dixon could hear her sobbing as she went.

'Your turn, Jon.'

He stepped forward and stood on the garden path, looking all around him.

'Face down on the lawn, Jon, arms outstretched. This is no time for mucking about,' said Dixon.

Jon turned to face Dixon and winked at him. Then he lay face down on the lawn with his arms in front of him. Two firearms officers ran over. They dragged his arms behind his back and handcuffed him.

'You prick,' said Dixon, 'I thought you were gonna . . .'

'Nah.'

Chapter Three

'Put them on Jan's desk for now,' said Dixon.

Jane and a police constable, who had been in the wrong place at the wrong time, had carried the boxes of Noel Woodman's belongings up to the office Dixon shared with DI Janice Courtenay on the second floor of Bridgwater Police Station.

'We'll have a quick rummage and then get them over to Scientific to see if they can find anything.'

Jane put on disposable rubber gloves and emptied the contents of the boxes onto the desk.

'Nothing of interest,' said Jane.

'What's of interest is what isn't here,' said Dixon.

'What do you mean?'

'Nothing of value. I mean at all.'

'Like what?'

'TV, radio, camera, iPad, iPod, computer. Nothing. You'd expect to find something like that, wouldn't you?'

'I suppose you would,' replied Jane.

'We need to ruffle a few feathers at that racing yard, I think. You saw the shifty looks and twitching curtains?'

'I did.'

DCI Lewis appeared in the doorway of Dixon's office.

'Well done, Nick.'

'Thank you, Sir. I don't think Mr Bateman was too chuffed about it . . .'

'I'll keep him off your back, don't worry. He was right, though. We are a bit thin on the ground at the moment. Dave Harding and Mark Pearce are still finishing off your last one.'

'What about Louise Willmott?'

'She was on secondment from uniform last time. Leave it with me.'

'Thank you, Sir.'

'I'm still taking a bit of a flyer leaving you two together, so don't let me down.'

'We won't, Sir,' replied Jane.

———‿———

Dixon switched on his computer and checked his email while Jane put Noel's belongings back in the boxes and arranged for them to be taken over to Scientific Services.

'I suppose you think you're bloody clever?'

The voice came from the doorway. Dixon looked over.

'And you are?'

'Harry Unwin. DS Harry Unwin.'

'And that's the way you usually address a senior officer, is it?' asked Dixon.

'You've made me look a right idiot.'

'And how did I do that, exactly?'

'You have no idea what you're dealing with. No fucking idea.'

Dixon looked back to his computer screen. 'I'm going to count to three and if you're still there when I've finished you're going to be in serious trouble. Do I make myself clear?'

Silence.

'One, two . . .'

'He's gone,' said Jane. 'I wonder what that was all about.'

'I don't know, Jane, but I have a feeling we'll find out.'

———

'Have you got it in for me or something?'

'C'mon, knee deep in horse shit has got to be better than the last one,' replied Dixon.

'True,' said Watson.

Donald Watson was the senior scenes of crime officer, as Dixon insisted on calling them. 'Scientific Services' didn't have the same ring to it and 'crime scene investigator' made Watson's job sound more exciting than his own. He declined the offer of a handshake but only because Watson's outstretched rubber gloved hand was covered in dung.

'Ah, sorry about that,' said Watson.

Dixon had counted three vans but could see only one team at work in Westbrook Warrior's stable.

'What did Lewis tell you?'

'That the body was found in here. I've got another team in the static caravan where he lived and another sifting through the muckheap for blood soaked straw.'

'Can we get the team off the muckheap for the time being?'

'Why?'

'He was killed somewhere else and then thrown in the stable. We need to find where. It may have been in the caravan, but at that time in the morning he'd have been out and about, getting ready for the day's racing.'

'So, it could be anywhere, is what you're saying?'

'I suppose it could,' replied Dixon.

'He was killed with a club with a horseshoe nailed to it. Right?' asked Jane.

'Yes.'

'So, that rules out a confined space, doesn't it? You wouldn't risk attacking someone in the dark without room to manoeuvre, would you?'

'Good thinking, Jane,' said Dixon. 'Start with the open spaces. The horses had been fed, according to the witness statements, so don't bother with the feed room either.'

'Or the tack room,' said Jane. 'It's too small.'

'It also rules out the stables and the alleyway,' said Watson.

'It does,' replied Dixon.

'Leave it with me.'

'Right then, Jane. Let's go and ruffle some feathers.'

Dixon and Jane walked up to the farmhouse. He gestured to four uniformed officers, who had been standing by, to follow them, and waited until they had caught up before ringing the doorbell. He also knocked on the large carved oak door for good measure. It was answered by Michael Hesp.

'Mr Hesp, may we have a word, please?'

'Er, yes. Come in.'

'Is Mrs Harcourt available?'

'Yes, we're in the kitchen. This way.'

Dixon followed Hesp along the corridor. It had a low ceiling and was dimly lit but he could make out an old flagstone floor. Doors either side, presumably to dining and living rooms, were closed.

It took a moment for Dixon's eyes to adjust to the brighter light in the kitchen, which was only marginally cleaner than one of the stables. Mrs Harcourt was sitting at the kitchen table, pulling hard on what was left of a cigarette. She had unkempt grey hair and looked older than her sixty years.

'Mrs Georgina Harcourt?'

'Yes.'

'I am Detective Insp—'

'I know who you are. We gave statements before.'

'Noel Woodman's death is now the subject of a murder investigation . . .'

'We told the other chap everything we know,' said Hesp.

'You answered all his questions?' asked Dixon.

'We did.'

'Well, I have more questions,' said Dixon, 'as you might imagine.'

'Let's get it over with, then,' said Mrs Harcourt.

'I'll need you both to accompany us to Bridgwater Police Station, please.'

'Do we have a choice?' asked Hesp.

Dixon turned and looked at the four uniformed officers standing behind him.

'I thought not,' said Hesp.

'Before we go, I'd just like to take the rest of Noel's belongings, if I may?' asked Dixon.

'The rest?'

'I think you know what I mean.'

Michael Hesp looked nervously at Mrs Harcourt. She shook her head and looked away.

'Wait here,' he said.

Dixon turned to one of the uniformed officers.

'Go with him.'

Hesp reappeared a few moments later carrying a holdall in his right hand and an iPad and a digital camera in his left, which he handed to Jane. He handed the holdall to Dixon.

'What's in here?'

'A PlayStation and some games.'

Dixon looked in the bag and then at Hesp.

'I don't know why I didn't give them to you when you were here before, really. Stupid, I know,' said Hesp.

The uniformed officers escorted Georgina Harcourt and Michael Hesp to separate police cars for the short drive to Bridgwater.

'Where are we going?' asked Jane.

Dixon took out his phone and rang the family liaison officer, Karen Marsden.

'Where's Natalie Woodman?'

'She's been to see her father at the hospital and is at home now. I'm here with her.'

'Thanks. We're on our way. I need a word with her.'

'OK.'

Dixon rang off.

'Home first, Jane. Then Pawlett.'

It was dark by the time they arrived at Manor Park in Pawlett. Monty was asleep in the back of the Land Rover, having been fed and given five minutes in the field behind Dixon's cottage. Dixon himself had used the opportunity to take some Tramadol, which made the seat belt over his left shoulder more tolerable. Lights were on in the other houses, which told him that the residents had been allowed home.

'You've got a new telly,' said Dixon.

'It's the one from upstairs.'

'Are you all right?'

'Yeah, fine.'

'And Leanne?'

'She's asleep.'

'What about your father?'

'He's going to be fine. Should be home tomorrow.'

'Good.'

'What will happen to Jon?'

'He'll be remanded in custody by the magistrates tomorrow and then go to Exeter Prison.'

'Neither of us will press charges.'

'That'll help him,' replied Dixon. 'Can we talk about Noel?'

'What do you want to know?'

'How old was he when your father threw him out?'

'It wasn't like that.'

'What was it like?'

'Dad didn't throw him out. He just made it impossible for him to stay.'

'So, Noel left?'

'He did.'

'And where did he go, what did he do?'

'He drifted around. Stayed with friends here, there and everywhere. It was impossible to keep up with him.'

'Did you keep in touch?'

'Tried to.'

'How?'

'Mobile phone and email. It was the only way.'

'Where's his phone, do you know?'

'It's here. I picked it up from the hospital, after he . . .' Her voice tailed off.

'I'll make some tea,' said Karen Marsden.

'Thanks,' replied Dixon. 'Can you get the phone, Natalie?'

'Yes. I've got his wallet too. Do you want that as well?'

'Yes, please.'

Karen Marsden brought the tea in just as Natalie returned with Noel's phone and wallet.

'Did you ever meet any of his friends, Natalie?' asked Dixon.

'Only one. An older man. He lived over near Glastonbury.'

'Name?'

'Philip, I think it was. Philip Stockman, or something like that.'

'How did they meet?'

'In a car park. That was the way Noel always met his friends.'

'What did Philip Stockman do for a living, can you remember?'

'He was an accountant.'

'So, tell me about his job at the racing stables . . .'

'It was Philip who had horses and got Noel involved, really. He loved it. He was a good rider, too. I've got a video clip on my computer of his first riding lesson.'

'Can you email it to me?'

'Yes. Then when Philip and Noel fell out, Noel got the job at Gidley's. That was about eighteen months ago.'

'Had you seen much of Noel since then?'

'He used to come over now and again when Dad was out. He didn't have a car, though, so it made it difficult.'

'And he never said anything to you about blowing the whistle on something big, as Jon put it?'

'No.'

'What about Jon, then? Did he talk to Noel often?'

'They kept in touch on Facebook and used FaceTime too.'

'OK, that's enough for now, I think.'

'Is that it?'

'It's early days, Natalie. We'll need to speak again, no doubt.'

'OK.'

Dixon handed her his card. 'Don't forget to email me that video clip.'

'I won't.'

Dixon sat in the Land Rover and opened Noel's wallet.

'A bank card.'

'I'll get statements, don't worry,' replied Jane.

'And the phone needs to go to High Tech.'

'I'll sort it.'

'Good. Let's get over to Bridgwater, then.'

They arrived at Bridgwater Police Station to find WPC Louise Willmott waiting for them in the CID room.

'Hello, Louise, are you with us?'

'Yes, Sir.'

'Right, get bank statements for this account and the phone, camera and iPad over to High Tech, please. I want all the numbers on the phone identified, calls made and received.' Dixon looked at his watch. 'And then be back here at 8 a.m. sharp.'

'Thank you, Sir.'

'You and me, Jane. Hesp first, then Mrs Harcourt.'

The interview with Michael Hesp began just after 7 p.m. Dixon cautioned him and reminded him that he was not under arrest and was free to leave at any time.

'But I'm guessing that wouldn't be wise?' asked Hesp.

'It would not,' replied Dixon. 'What can you tell me about the death of Noel Woodman?'

'Nothing, really.' He shook his head. 'Nothing that I haven't already said. I heard the shout from Kevin at about 5.30 a.m., threw my clothes on and ran out to find Noel dead in Westbrook Warrior's stable.'

'No noise or anything before that?'

'I was asleep.'

'We have reason to believe that Noel was about to blow the whistle on something. Any ideas what that might have been, Mr Hesp?'

'No. None at all.'

'Something big, apparently.'

'Nope.'

'Because when you think of a groom at a racing yard blowing the whistle you think of doping, for example.'

'Certainly not. I've never done anything like that.'

'What about your results?'

'We may not win as much as we should, but we race clean.'

'Really?'

'The horses are tested, for heaven's sake. You can check, if you don't believe me.'

'I intend to.'

'Our vet and the British Horseracing Authority,' said Hesp.

Jane wrote down the name and address of the veterinary surgeon.

'We're completely clean. Always have been.'

'So why do you think someone might wish to murder your groom, then?'

'I thought it was an accident.'

'Sadly, not. But someone went to a great deal of trouble to make it look like one.'

'How?' asked Hesp.

'You tell me,' replied Dixon.

'I really don't know.'

'Why did you have Westbrook Warrior's shoes removed?'

'Safety.'

'And you can think of no reason why someone would want to kill Noel.'

'No.'

'What did you think of his lifestyle?'

'What he did in his own time was up to him.'

'And the PlayStation and other stuff?'

'What about them?'

'How did he afford it all?'

'No idea.'

'How much did you pay him?'

'Five pounds an hour. Cash.'

'Below the minimum wage . . .'

'He got free board and lodging into the bargain.'

'What were you going to do with them?'

'I had some crazy notion to sell them on eBay when the dust had settled, if I'm being honest.'

'Tell me about the race day routine.'

'The horses are fed first, then mucked out while they're eating. That's as far as Noel had got that day but usually they'd be groomed and then got ready for travelling.'

'Which involves?'

'Tails plaited and covered, leg bandages, rugs, that sort of thing.'

'And when are you racing again?'

'Tomorrow. We've got two going at Exeter.'

'One last question. You said when you heard Kevin Tanner's shout you threw your clothes on and ran out.'

'Yes.'

'So, you live in the farmhouse?'

'Yes, I do. But, no, Mrs Harcourt and I are not a couple, if that's where you're going with this.'

'You have your own room?'

'Yes.'

'And you were in it on your own?'

'Yes.'

'Would Mrs Harcourt be able to confirm your whereabouts, then?'

'An alibi, you mean?'

'That's exactly what I mean,' replied Dixon.

'I doubt it. Her room is at the back of the house and she sometimes takes sleeping pills, too.'

'Thank you, Mr Hesp. You may as well wait while we speak to Mrs Harcourt and then a car will take you home.'

'Fine.'

———

The interview with Georgina Harcourt was over in less than ten minutes. She said that she played no part whatsoever in the running of the racing yard, although she did help Hesp with the paperwork from time to time. Otherwise, her involvement was limited to leasing the whole premises to Michael Hesp for his training business. She found it far easier and more lucrative than running her own livery yard, as she had done in the past with her late husband. Hesp was also her lodger.

On the morning of Noel's death the police were already on the scene by the time she got out of bed. She said that she had only spoken to Noel on perhaps three or four occasions in all the time he had been there and she could think of no one who might wish to kill him.

Dixon terminated the interview just after 8 p.m. and Jane arranged for a car to take Mrs Harcourt and Hesp back to Spaxton.

———

Dixon was sitting at his computer, watching the clip of Noel's first riding lesson that Natalie had emailed to him, when his phone rang. It was Donald Watson.

'I think you'd better get over here, Nick.'

'We're on our way, Don.'

He met Jane on the stairs.

'SOCO have come up with something.'

'I'll get my handbag.'

They drove west out of Bridgwater towards Durleigh Reservoir. It was a dark November night, with broken cloud racing across the sky on a strong south westerly wind. Dixon watched the moonlight shimmering on the water.

They drove through Spaxton, past the Lamb Inn, and arrived at the racing stables to find the whole yard lit by arc lamps. A large area was cordoned off and various smaller areas marked on the ground with white tape. Kevin Tanner was going from stable to stable feeding the horses, all except Westbrook Warrior, whose stable was still empty.

'Where is he?' asked Dixon.

'We moved him round into the barn,' replied Watson.

'Give me a minute.'

Dixon walked around the area that had been cordoned off and along the alleyway between the stables and the hay barn. He went into the American barn. Both sides were lined with stables, twelve in total, each sectioned off with wood panelling to five feet high and then steel bars on top.

He walked along until he recognised Westbrook Warrior. He was at the far end on the right. This time there was no metal grille in place and the Warrior's head was out over the stable door. Dixon knew that the horse was watching him approach.

He heard footsteps behind him. Jane was running to catch up.

'What are you doing?'

'I just want to check something.'

They approached the stable. Westbrook Warrior stepped back inside and ripped a large mouthful of haylage from his net and then put his head back over the door. Dixon watched him eating.

'What?' asked Jane.

Dixon inched forward and stood by the latch on the stable door, within reach of the Warrior's head. The horse stared at him.

'Be careful.'

'It's all right, Jane. His ears are up. Maybe he's not such a . . .'

Suddenly, Westbrook Warrior's ears went flat back on the top of his head. Dixon saw it and stepped back just as the Warrior lunged at him, baring his teeth. Dixon stumbled backwards but kept his footing.

'No, he is aggressive. Make a note to get his records from the vet tomorrow, will you?'

Jane was laughing so much she couldn't reply.

'For heaven's sake, Constable, get a grip,' said Dixon.

'Right then, what've we got?'

'This way,' said Watson. He lifted the blue tape that was cordoning off an area outside the last two stables in the block and stepped under it. Dixon and Jane followed.

'It was raining heavily when he was killed and it's rained since, of course, but we've got the residue of a large pool of blood here,' said Watson, pointing to an area on the concrete plinth in front of the stables. 'There's some light spatter on the brickwork, too, and then a trail of blood running along the gutter into that drain you can see over there. There's some on the block paving, too. It's not visible to the naked eye, of course.'

'Anything else?'

'Yes. He'd been mucking out at the time so we checked the wheelbarrows. That one has blood spatter on the handles. Not much, but enough. You can see it in the rust.'

Dixon looked at an old wheelbarrow that was standing under cover in the hay barn.

'What about the muckheap?' asked Dixon.

'That's next.'

'So, he was killed there . . .'

'Looks like it,' said Watson.

'And then carried, what, ten paces to Westbrook Warrior's stable and thrown in?'

'It's not much further than that,' said Jane.

'The killer then washed the plinth off with the hose over there,' said Dixon, pointing to a yellow hose coiled around an outside tap on the wall of the feed room.

'Looks like it, yes,' said Watson.

'Thanks, Don,' said Dixon, 'are you gonna be here all night?'

'As long as it takes.'

Dixon and Jane ducked under the blue tape and walked across the yard towards the car park. Dixon looked up at the farmhouse to see Georgina Harcourt watching them from the window. She turned away when she saw him looking at her.

'Let's try the Lamb in the village, Jane. We've just got time to get there before they stop serving food.'

Dixon took two Tramadol with a large swig of Doom Bar.

'Are you sure you should be doing that?'

'One pint'll be all right. Don't panic. It'll help me sleep.'

'I won't need any help with that,' replied Jane. 'It's been a bloody long day.'

'Let's focus on what we know, then,' said Dixon.

'Like what?'

'Not the detail, I mean. What it tells us.'

'What?'

'Noel was killed by someone who doesn't know the difference between a standard horseshoe and a racing plate, for starters.'

'Yes, that figures.'

'And in this game that must narrow it down, surely?'

'It must.'

'And yet someone who knew that he'd be out and about on his own at that time in the morning . . .'

'True.'

'. . . On a race day.'

Jane nodded. 'Someone who thought Noel was about to expose them for something big, if Jon's right about that,' she said.

'Good point,' replied Dixon.

'And that Westbrook Warrior's an aggressive little devil?'

'Meaning that his stable was the right one to leave the body in so it wouldn't arouse suspicion.'

'Exactly,' said Jane.

'So, they know some things but not others . . .'

Dixon looked up. A waitress was standing next to their table in the corner of the bar, holding two plates of scampi and chips.

Chapter Four

Dixon was asleep before Jane pulled out of the car park at the Lamb Inn. He woke up when they got home, but only for as long as it took him to get from the car into bed.

This time he slept straight through the night, the effect of the Tramadol and beer negated by his tiredness. He had been on the go since 3 a.m. that morning, almost twenty hours, but it had, at least, taken his mind off the pain in his left shoulder.

He woke just before 7 a.m. and made coffee and toast for Jane, which he carried up to her on a tray.

'Breakfast in bed?' she said, rubbing her eyes. 'What have I done to deserve this?'

'Nothing.'

'Where's your sling?'

'I'm going to try it without now. It feels a lot better.'

'Good.'

'I'm just going to take Monty round the back.'

Dixon opened the back door and watched as Monty tore around the back of his Land Rover, under the fence and into the field at the back of the cottage. Dixon followed, climbing over the fence with an umbrella in his right hand. He stood in the corner of the field, deep in thought. Who would know not much, but enough? About race day routine and Westbrook Warrior's aggression, but not about his shoes? And what about a motive? Assuming Jon was right and Noel was about to blow the whistle on something, what was it?

He watched Monty sniffing along the hedge.

Denials from Georgina Harcourt and Hesp. To be expected and taken with a pinch of salt. But then both would have known a racing plate from a . . .

'Are you coming in? We have to go in a minute,' shouted Jane.

. . . standard shoe. He was convinced they were hiding something. There had been something about their denials. A little too rehearsed, perhaps? Certainly, Hesp was unreliable. He wasn't quite so sure about Georgina Harcourt, though.

———

Louise Willmott was waiting for them when they arrived at Bridgwater Police Station.

'It's still just us, then?' asked Dixon.

'Looks like it, Sir,' replied Louise.

'My office. Janice is on a trial in Bristol for the next week or so.'

Louise sat down at Janice Courtenay's desk and Jane on the chair in front of Dixon's desk.

'We'll use this whiteboard,' he said, turning to the board on the wall behind his desk. He pinned up a photograph of Noel and then turned round to see DCI Lewis standing in the doorway.

'Don't mind me. Saves you going through it all twice.'

'Yes, Sir.'

Dixon turned back to the whiteboard. 'Noel Woodman. We're supposed to believe that he was kicked to death by Westbrook Warrior, a horse that's known to be aggressive. He was found in his stable covered in marks made by a horseshoe like this one.'

Dixon handed the heavy steel shoe to Louise.

'There are three problems with that. Firstly, Westbrook Warrior wasn't wearing shoes like this. He was wearing racing plates, like these.'

He passed the aluminium plate to Jane, who passed it to Louise.

'Secondly, the marks on the body suggest that round nails had been used and farrier's nails have square heads, so it hadn't been attached to a horse's hoof, that's for sure. My money's on a piece of wood.'

'And the third problem?' asked Louise.

'There's the imprint of only one shoe on the body.' Dixon paused. 'And horses have four legs, as we know. At the very least, you'd expect two, depending on whether the horse attacked with its front or back legs.'

'Anything else?' asked Lewis.

'SOCO have found a large area of blood spatter on the concrete plinth outside and ten or so paces along from Westbrook Warrior's stable. There was also blood on a wheelbarrow. They were still working on it when we left them to it late last night, but it looks like that's where he was killed and the body was then thrown in the stable. I'm still awaiting final reports from Roger Poland and SOCO.'

'Was the wheelbarrow used to move the body?' asked Louise.

'It's possible, but it's light spatter consistent with him being attacked while pushing it along, I think. It's a good point, though, Louise.'

Dixon glared at Jane.

'The farrier confirms the detail and that the horse is aggressive. I can vouch for that too.'

'He got a bit too close,' said Jane.

'We've spoken to the yard owner, Georgina Harcourt, and also the trainer, Michael Hesp. He rents the premises from Mrs Harcourt. Neither has an alibi but otherwise they denied everything.'

'Everything?' asked Lewis.

'Yes, Sir.'

'What about Jon Woodman's statement that his brother was going to blow the whistle?'

'We're working on it. Both Georgina Harcourt and Michael Hesp said they had no idea what that might be about.'

'Well, they would, wouldn't they?' said Louise.

'True,' replied Dixon.

'Well, it sounds like you've got your work cut out, Nick. I'm sorry I can't offer more help,' said Lewis, looking at his watch. 'I've got a meeting in . . .'

'That's all right, Sir, we'll manage.'

'Good. Keep me posted.'

DCI Lewis turned on his heels and was gone.

'Three coffees, I think, Louise. One sugar for me, please.'

'Yes, Sir.'

Jane waited until Louise had gone to the coffee machine.

'What's the matter?'

'Why didn't I spot that about the wheelbarrow being used to move the body?'

'It could be . . .'

'It's these bloody painkillers, that's what it is. You'll have to watch me.'

'You'll be fine.'

'My brain doesn't function . . .'

Louise arrived back with two coffees in plastic cups.

'You not having one, Louise?' asked Jane.

'No, thanks.'

'Right, let's get on,' said Dixon. 'I want more evidence that he was killed elsewhere and thrown in the stable. Jane, get onto Roger Poland and see if we can get the dung samples tested.'

'The ones taken from Noel's nose and mouth?'

'Yes. We need to know whether it contains Dodson & Horrell Racehorse Cubes or Mix. If it's Mix, it's not Westbrook Warrior's.'

'Yes, Sir.'

'Louise, we need to know everything about Noel. Background, the lot. Chase up his bank statements and High Tech, will you? We need to know what's on his iPad and phone. Find his former partner, too.'

'Name?'

'Philip Stockman. An accountant from Glastonbury way.'

'Yes, Sir.'

'And I want a complete list of all of the owners of the horses trained by Hesp. All individuals and syndicate members.'

'Yes, Sir.'

'Jane, I want Westbrook Warrior's veterinary records. And accounts and bank statements for Hesp's training business.'

'OK.'

'Find out who rides for him, too.'

'Jockeys, you mean?'

'Yes. Get onto the Jockey Club and find out what you can about them.'

'Will do.'

Dixon sat at his desk and powered up his computer.

'We'll find you an empty desk out here, Louise,' said Jane, on her way out to the open plan area of the CID Room.

Louise Willmott got up and followed her just as DC Mark Pearce appeared in the doorway.

'You're looking well, Sir.'

'Thanks, Mark.'

'How's the arm?'

'It'll be fine.'

'We do still need your statement . . .'

Dixon's blank expression told Pearce he needed a reminder.

'Last Sunday. The Allandale Lodge. You got stabbed . . . ?'

Dixon shook his head.

'Yes, of course. Leave it with me. If I dictate it can you get it typed up?'

'Yes, no problem.'

'Sorry, Mark. I've been a bit . . .'

'So I'm told, Sir. Have fun.'

'Thanks.'

Dixon's last case had been an unusual one. It was the first time he had been confronted with a severed head and, whilst he had brought the investigation to a satisfactory conclusion without further loss of life, he had paid a high price for it. He looked down at his left shoulder. The physical scar would soon be gone and he hoped the others would soon follow. Maybe when he stopped taking the damn painkillers and got a decent night's sleep.

He logged in to the police network and checked his email. Nothing of interest. Then he opened Internet Explorer and searched Google for the British Horseracing Authority. He clicked on 'Contact Us' and then dialled the number.

'BHA. How can I help you?'

'My name is Detective Inspector Dixon. Avon and Somerset CID. I am investigating a murder at a racing stables in Somerset and need to speak to someone about them.'

'About the stables?'

'Yes. I need to know if there are any regulatory or disciplinary issues outstanding, any current or past investigations, that sort of thing.'

'That'll be Integrity Services and Licensing. Please hold.'

Dixon held the phone away from his ear. He hated listening to music when on hold.

'Hello?'

Dixon explained again who he was and why he was calling.

'Where's this yard, again?'

'Spaxton, Somerset.'

'That'll be Adam Spiers you need to speak to. He's in a meeting at the moment. Can I get him to call you?'

'Yes, please do. It's very urgent.'

Dixon left his telephone numbers, office and mobile, and then fetched himself another coffee from the machine. He spent the next twenty minutes searching Google for anything and everything he could find about Michael Hesp and Gidley's Racing Stables. He found nothing of real interest except for a thread on a betting forum, where the general consensus seemed to be that Hesp's horses were to be avoided unless laying to lose. Dixon made a mental note to do some research into laying to lose. It was not a term that he was familiar with and that always made him uncomfortable.

Then he reached for his Dictaphone and spent the next two hours dictating two witness statements, the first dealing with events at the Allandale Lodge Care Home the previous Sunday morning and the second setting out the events of the Tuesday night inside 37 Manor Park.

He had just finished when his phone rang. He checked his watch. It was just after 11 a.m.

'Nick Dixon.'

'Adam Spiers. British Horseracing Integrity Services. I gather you wanted a word about a racing yard at Spaxton.'

'Yes, Gidley's Racing Stables. The trainer is Michael Hesp . . .'

'The message said there's been a murder?'

'One of the grooms was found dead,' replied Dixon.

'Is this the lad who was kicked by the colt?'

'Yes and no. He was dead before he was thrown into the stable.'

'Bloody hell.'

'What can you tell me about Michael Hesp?'

'Well, I'm not sure I can . . .'

'This is a murder investigation, Mr Spiers.'

'Yes, of course. He runs a reasonable operation. The horses are well looked after, so there are no equine welfare issues for us to worry about. We have been looking at his results in the last eighteen months or so, though.'

'What does that mean exactly?'

'We've been looking at irregular betting patterns. We monitor live betting in real time and there have been several suspicious episodes, shall we say?'

'Is Hesp aware of this?'

'Yes, we had him in for interview in July, I think it was. He denied everything.'

'Where are you based?'

'Newmarket.'

'Shame. I was hoping to meet . . .'

'I'm going to be in our London office tomorrow, if that's any good to you?'

'It is.'

'I have two hours clear before lunch, say, 11 a.m.?'

'See you then.'

'I'll bring the file,' said Spiers.

'I can get a court order for its release if that would assist?'

'No, it's fine. I expect the police would have been getting involved sooner or later anyway,' said Spiers.

Dixon put the phone down and shouted at the open door of his office.

'Jane.'

He was about to shout again when Jane appeared in the doorway.

'Yes, Sir.'

'We need two tickets to London tomorrow morning. We'll pick up the fast train at Taunton. There's one eightish that gets in tennish.'

'Where are we going?'

'To meet a British Horseracing Authority Integrity Services officer. They've been investigating irregular betting patterns on some of Hesp's horses, it seems.'

'Really? You have been busy.'

'I have. Then get your coat. We're off to the races.'

'So, Hesp lied,' said Jane.

'He did. But then he denied it when interviewed by the BHA as well.'

'And he got away with it that time, I suppose?'

'We'll find out tomorrow. He's still being monitored by them, from what I can gather, but we'll see.'

'What's an irregular betting pattern, I wonder?'

'We'll find that out, too. Either way, we've got a possible motive,' said Dixon.

'Possible?'

'Assuming that's what Noel was going to blow the whistle about, yes.'

'What else could it have been?'

'No idea. But we can't jump to conclusions.'

Dixon checked the glove box of the Land Rover for his binoculars as they crossed the River Exe on the M5.

'We've got time for some lunch. Get off at Kennford and we'll try that pub at the bottom of the hill.'

Jane turned off the M5 at the foot of Haldon Hill and into The Gissons. They took an hour over lunch and then spent twenty minutes in the woods with Monty, arriving at Exeter Racecourse just before 2 p.m. Dixon had checked the racecard online and knew that Hesp had two horses going, Midnight Blue in the 2.40 p.m. and Uphill Tobermory in the 3.10 p.m. They bought two tickets on the gate and walked across to the grandstand. It was cloudy and dry, with a strong south westerly wind. Perfect racing weather, according to the man in the ticket booth.

'Fancy a flutter, Jane?'

'Should we?'

'No, we shouldn't, you're right.' Dixon winked at her. 'Let's find the Betting Ring.'

Jane followed.

'You done this before?' asked Dixon.

'Once or twice on the Grand National but that's it.'

'Me too. I'm sure there must be a more scientific way of doing it than whether I like the name.'

They walked around the side of the grandstand. Dixon noticed the Parade Ring off to the right, where the horses going in the 2.10 p.m. were being walked around. He could see the stables and various horse lorries behind that. To his left was the grandstand with the Betting Ring in front. Dixon counted eighteen on course bookmakers, each standing underneath a large and brightly coloured umbrella.

The course itself was laid out on the top of Haldon Hill with the traditional white rails stretching off into the distance. It was completely encircled by trees and appeared to undulate, making it uphill and downhill in parts. The long finishing straight was off to the right of the grandstand.

'It's a bloody long way round,' said Jane.

'Let's get a drink,' said Dixon.

He picked up a copy of the *Racing Post* that had been left lying on the bar. It was already open at the Exeter racecard.

'I wonder what all these numbers mean?' said Dixon.

'Here, let me,' said the barman. He pointed to one of the horses. 'That's the age. That's the weight it's carrying and that's its recent results. Trainer and jockey. The latest odds are on the screens, or you can get them from the on course bookmakers out front.'

'What's the "P", then?'

'Pulled up.'

'Which makes the "F" fell?'

'That's it.'

'What are these?'

'That's the Official Rating and that's the Racing Post Rating. They're based on the form.'

'What's the significance of the weight?'

'In a handicap, the more weight it's carrying, the better the horse. That's the handicap.'

'Thank you.'

'Good luck.'

Dixon looked at the racecard for the 2.40 p.m. Midnight Blue was five years old and carrying more weight than the other horses in the race. His last five results were 4U3/22.

'What's the "U"?' asked Jane.

'Unseated rider, I suppose.'

'So, he's finished second in his last two races?'

'He has.'

'The jockey is S McCarthy, it says.'

'That's Sam,' replied Jane. 'I'm waiting to hear from the Jockey Club about him.'

'Let's check the odds.'

Dixon walked over and stood in front of one of the wall mounted screens.

'He's the favourite. Two to one.'

'What does that mean?'

'I bet a quid and get two if he wins. Plus I get my quid back.'

'What's seven to two then?'

'I suppose it's the equivalent of three point five to one,' said Dixon.

The second favourite was called Hogan's Missile at odds of seven to two. His results were similar to Midnight Blue's although he had, at least, finished each race.

'Which one are you going to go for?'

'Well, Hesp's rarely win, by all accounts, so I'll go for Hogan's Missile, I think.'

They stood in the window of the bar and watched the 2.10 p.m. There was one faller but both horse and rider got straight to their feet.

'Let's get down to the Betting Ring.'

They walked around the ring until Dixon found the best odds on Hogan's Missile. One bookmaker was offering four to one and Dixon placed ten pounds on the horse to win. He turned to Jane.

'We need to get somewhere we can see the Parade Ring.'

Dixon watched through his binoculars from in front of the grandstand. He could see Kevin Tanner leading Midnight Blue towards the Parade Ring. Behind them walked Michael Hesp. He was wearing tweed.

He watched Tanner take out his mobile phone and dial a number, before putting the phone to his right ear. At precisely the same moment, Dixon heard a phone ringing in front of him, down amongst the on course bookmakers in the Betting Ring. It was answered by a large man standing under an orange and white umbrella. The sign on his stand read J Clapham Racing. Dixon looked from one to the other. The synchronisation of Tanner and the man speaking and listening was perfect and they both rang off at the same time. Dixon was convinced they had been speaking to each other.

The man turned around and began typing on a keyboard out of Dixon's eyeline. Dixon watched through his binoculars and noticed Midnight Blue's odds on the black and orange LED display change from two to one to four to one. Dixon was astonished at how quickly a small queue then formed.

'Got your notebook, Jane?' asked Dixon.

'Yes.'

'Make a note, will you? Kevin Tanner's mobile phone records and J Clapham Racing. We need to speak to both of them too.'

The horses left the Parade Ring and made their way out onto the course. Dixon could feel his pulse quicken. Midnight Blue's colours were light blue with a large white circle in the middle. Hogan's Missile's were red and black squares, much like Dixon's old school rugby shirt.

Then they were off.

Dixon followed the horses through his binoculars. He lost them briefly in a dip on the far side of the course but they soon came back into view heading up towards the turn in the far corner. A lone horse was four lengths clear with both Midnight Blue and Hogan's Missile in the chasing pack.

As they came off the final bend, Midnight Blue and Hogan's Missile had caught the front runner and all three were neck and neck.

'Which one's yours?' asked Jane.

'Red and black,' replied Dixon. He passed Jane the binoculars.

'He's winning.'

'Easy money,' said Dixon.

By the time they jumped the final hurdle, Hogan's Missile was two lengths clear and he pulled even further away on the home straight. Dixon thought it a bit of an anticlimax.

'C'mon Jane, let's rattle Hesp's cage and see what happens.'

'Aren't you going to collect your winnings?'

Dixon took the betting slip out of his pocket and looked at the name on the top: J Clapham Racing. He screwed the slip into a tight ball and threw it on the ground.

'No,' he said.

They stood on the far side of the Parade Ring, right by the railings, so that Hesp and Tanner would see them as they led Uphill Tobermory from the stables at the back.

'Tell you what, Jane. You go back to the Betting Ring and keep a close eye on J Clapham Racing. I want to know if he gets a phone call and what he does.'

'Right.'

Dixon turned to see the horses getting ready for the next race. He could see Kevin Tanner holding a large grey horse. Michael Hesp was helping the jockey up into the saddle. Then they turned and joined the back of the line of horses walking out to the Parade Ring.

'Good afternoon, Mr Hesp,' said Dixon. 'Bad luck in the last race.'

'Thank you,' said Hesp, turning to face Dixon. The blood drained from his face when he recognised him. He looked away and ran a few steps to catch up with Kevin Tanner, who was leading Uphill Tobermory.

Dixon stepped back from the railings and disappeared into the crowd, at the same time keeping a close eye on both Hesp and Tanner. Both looked around to where Dixon had been standing and then appeared to scan the crowd looking for him. Hesp then spoke to the jockey and Tanner reached for his telephone.

Dixon made his way over to the front of the grandstand where Jane was watching the Betting Ring.

'Well?'

'His phone rang. A short conversation then he changed the odds on Uphill Tobermory from four to one to two to one,' replied Jane.

Dixon looked through his binoculars at J Clapham Racing, who was now sitting at a laptop computer under the umbrella.

'He's on the Bet29 website,' said Dixon.

'What's he doing?' asked Jane.

'I don't know,' replied Dixon. 'Which pocket did he take his phone from when it rang?'

'Left coat pocket,' replied Jane.

Dixon rang the mobile phone number on the J Clapham Racing sign and waited. He could hear it ringing and watched as J Clapham reached into his right pocket and took out a telephone. Dixon rang off.

'Two phones,' he said.

'And they're off,' said Jane.

Dixon looked up to see the horses in the 3.10 p.m. set off in a clockwise direction around the track.

'If I was a betting man, I'd put my money on Uphill Tobermory winning this one,' said Dixon.

The race unfolded much as the last had done, with one horse several lengths clear for much of the early stages before slowly being caught by the chasing pack. As they came off the final bend, two were clear of the field and neck and neck. One was the big grey, Uphill Tobermory.

Dixon passed his binoculars to Jane. Uphill Tobermory stumbled at the second to last hurdle but was still able catch the leader and cross the line in first place by the narrowest of margins.

'You're right, this is easy money,'

'Only if you cheat,' replied Dixon.

They stayed for the last race at 3.50 p.m., but only so that Dixon could watch the panic unfold in Hesp's stables. Both of his horses were certified fit to travel by the vet and had been loaded on the lorry before the last race had even got under way. They were travelling north on the A38 before it had finished.

Neither Dixon nor Jane picked the winner of the last race.

'That's what happens when you don't have insider information, Jane,' said Dixon.

'And why it's a mug's game, I suppose?'

'Precisely. But if you know what's going to happen, there's a lot of money to be made, isn't there?'

'No shit.'

'Let's get out of here,' said Dixon.

'Back to the station?'

'No, home. I fancy an early night,' replied Dixon.

Jane smiled.

It was dark and pouring with rain by the time they reached Bridgwater on the M5. Dixon had been deep in thought for most of the drive north.

'Have you heard the phrase "laying to lose" before, Jane?'

'No.'

'Me neither.'

'What are you thinking?' she asked.

'Irregular betting patterns and horses that rarely win. The two must be connected, but how do you make money out of holding your horses back?'

'No idea.'

'Either you bet on the joint or second favourite winning or it's this laying to lose thing.'

'Or both.'

'Funny that Hesp's horse won when he knew we were watching, isn't it?'

'Very.'

'And Tanner's clearly got something going on the side with J Clapham Racing. It could be that Noel was going to . . .'

'Either that or he was doing it too, don't forget,' said Jane.

'Yes. Clapham would lose his licence if it came out.'

'At the very least.'

'And where the bloody hell did the money come from for that iPad and camera, I wonder?'

'And the PlayStation, don't forget.'

'That's fifteen hundred quid's worth.'

'Maybe he was still selling himself?' asked Jane.

'Maybe he was,' replied Dixon. 'Either way, we need to know where his money was coming from because it sure as hell wasn't coming from his wages, was it?'

'No.'

They arrived at Dixon's cottage just after 5.30 p.m. Jane went for a shower while Dixon fed Monty and then opened his laptop. He clicked on Internet Explorer and searched Google for 'laying to lose'. He scrolled down through the results and clicked on 'fivewinners.com'. He was still reading their 'Free Guide To Laying Horses' when Jane got out of the shower. She tiptoed up behind him, wrapped in her towel. Her blonde shoulder length hair was wet and straggly, freed of its usual ponytail.

'Are you coming to bed?'

'I'm not tired yet,' said Dixon.

'Who said anything about sleeping?'

'Oh, right,' replied Dixon, shutting the lid of his computer.

Dixon lay in the dark listening to the sound of Jane breathing. She was dozing next to him, her head on his pillow. He leaned over and kissed her on the forehead.

'What is it?' she said, stirring.

'We need to take that dog out and get something to eat.'

Monty had long since given up scratching at the door and gone back downstairs.

'We do,' replied Jane.

'How about the Red Cow?'

'Sounds good to me.'

'Did you find out what laying to lose is?' asked Jane.

They were sitting at their usual table in the corner of the lounge bar at the Red Cow. Monty was stretched out on the floor by their feet.

'Yes. Stick with me for a minute. Imagine a high street bookmaker. You walk in and back Midnight Blue for ten quid at odds of two to one. You place the bet and the bookie accepts it. Are you with me so far?'

'Yes.'

'If Midnight Blue wins, the bookie returns your stake to you and pays you twenty quid winnings. If Midnight Blue loses, he keeps your stake. Right?'

'Right.'

'Now, imagine yourself standing behind the counter in the bookmaker's shop. I come in and want to back Midnight Blue for ten quid and you want to accept that bet because you think Midnight Blue will lose. OK?'

Jane nodded.

'So, now, if Midnight Blue wins, you return my stake to me and pay me my winnings. If Midnight Blue loses, you keep my stake.'

'Still with me?'

'Yes.'

'Well, that's how laying to lose works. You can only do it on the online betting exchanges, websites like Bet29, but it means you can act as the bookie and accept bets others want to place.'

'So, if you know the horse is going to lose . . .'

'You can clean up. Exactly.'

'And that's the irregular betting patterns?'

'We'll find out tomorrow, but it must be. It would explain why Hesp's horses never win, wouldn't it?'

Chapter Five

Dixon spent most of the journey watching the world flash by. Jane dozed and listened to music, apart from the occasional trip to the buffet car. They had left his Land Rover at Taunton Station and caught the fast train to London, arriving just after 10 a.m. Jane looked at her watch.

'On time.'

'Near enough,' replied Dixon.

He had never liked travelling by train and it had been some time since it had last been forced on him. It was the feeling of not being in control at high speed. He always insisted on sitting with his back to the direction of travel so that if the train crashed he would not be cut in half by the table. He was also convinced that the available leg room had reduced dramatically since his last trip. They had at least had the table to themselves as far as Reading.

One question had troubled Dixon for much of the journey. Noel had worked for Hesp for eighteen months, according to his sister, Natalie, so he must have known about the betting scam for some time and been an active participant in it. It's possible he was even making a few quid on the side, as Kevin Tanner appeared to be doing. It would explain the iPad and PlayStation. If that was right, why threaten to blow the whistle on it now? Dixon had to consider the troubling possibility that it was not the motive for Noel's murder.

'Let's take the Tube.'

'I thought you didn't like travelling by train?'

'Tubes are different.' It struck Dixon as odd, even as he said it, but it was true. He did enjoy the London Underground and put it down to an old film with Donald Pleasence as a detective inspector investigating a series of gruesome murders on the Tube. He thought it best not to tell Jane about it.

They got on the Bakerloo Line and changed onto the Central Line at Oxford Circus. Holborn Station was only two stops along, so they stood for the short ride. Dixon was holding the handrail with his left hand.

'Your arm's better, then?' asked Jane.

Dixon looked down at his left shoulder.

'I suppose it must be, yes. A bit.'

The London office of the British Horseracing Authority was at 75 High Holborn. They walked along until they reached two glass doors between a coffee shop with an exotic name Dixon didn't recognise and a pub called the Red Lion. He looked at his watch. It was 10.30 a.m.

'Too early for the pub. Let's try the coffee.'

They sat in the window, Jane with a latte and Dixon a hot chocolate. He hadn't had breakfast and needed the sugar.

'Let's assume for a minute that the betting thing is not the motive for Noel's murder . . . ?'

'Yes.'

'What else could it have been?'

'Sex,' said Jane.

'Sex?'

'Well, it could've been, couldn't it? He was a rent boy, after all.'

'Go on.'

'Maybe he was blackmailing someone, or threatening to?'

Dixon thought about what Jon Woodman had said in the early hours of the previous Tuesday morning.

'He knew something and was going to go public with it . . . something big . . .'

'Who said that?' asked Jane.

'That's what Jon told me Noel had said to him.'

'And that's all he said?'

'Yes. They were on Skype. Jon was in Afghanistan.'

'Could mean anything, that,' replied Jane.

'It could.'

Dixon finished the dregs of his hot chocolate.

'C'mon, let's get next door.'

The offices of the British Horseracing Authority were on the second floor and, once past the security guard, Dixon and Jane took the lift. They were met by an outstretched hand when the doors opened.

'Adam Spiers. Did you have a good trip up?'

'Yes, thank you. I'm Nick Dixon and this is Detective Constable Jane Winter.'

They shook hands with Spiers and then produced their warrant cards.

'Follow me,' said Spiers.

They walked past the reception area and into a large interview room on the left. Dixon doubted that Spiers had worn a pin striped suit just for them and wondered what his other meetings were about that day. Spiers himself was in his forties with thick dark hair. He clearly enjoyed his food too.

'Coffee or tea?'

'Tea would be lovely,' said Jane. 'The coffee next door was . . .'

'Ah, sorry, should've warned you about that.'

'Tea for me too, please,' said Dixon.

Spiers picked up the telephone on the table.

'Sonia, could we have three teas in here, please? Thanks.' He replaced the handset and turned to Dixon and Jane. 'Tell me about the murder, then.'

'I'm afraid I'm limited in what I can say at this stage, as I'm sure you'll appreciate. Suffice it to say that Noel was dead before he was thrown into the stable and a good deal of effort had gone into making it look like the horse had kicked him to death.'

'Really. And do you have a motive?'

'It's early days, but we have reason to believe that he was about to go public with some information and that may be why he was killed.'

'What information, I wonder?'

'At the moment we don't know, but one possibility is the irregular betting patterns you mentioned when we spoke yesterday, of course. We thought about possible doping, too, but Michael Hesp insisted he was clean.'

'He is. We do regular checks for that, as you'd expect. He's not so squeaky clean when it comes to betting.'

'Go on,' said Dixon.

'How much do you know about backing and laying?' asked Spiers.

'We're learning fast but treat us as beginners for these purposes.'

'OK. Well, everything changed with the advent of the Internet betting exchanges. Bet29 and such like. Back in the old days you could only back a horse to win with a traditional bookmaker, either on course or on the high street.'

Jane was making notes.

'Now you can go online and effectively be the bookmaker. Not only can you back a horse to win but you can accept someone else's bet to win if you think the horse is going to lose. That's laying. It's a risky business, though.'

'How so?'

'A traditional bookie is laying all of the horses in the race, isn't he?'

'I suppose he is,' replied Dixon.

'And he does so at odds guaranteed to give him a profit whichever horse wins. OK?'

'Yes.'

'But if you're laying on the betting exchanges, the likelihood is you'll be laying just the one horse, and if it wins, you could be in deep shit.'

Dixon nodded.

'Let me give you an example. Take a horse at odds of eight to one. You lay it for a tenner. If it loses, you keep the backer's tenner. But if it wins, you pay out eighty quid, which is a big hole in your bank.'

'Why take the risk, then?' asked Dixon.

'OK, well, let's say you have a race with nine runners. If you're trying to back the winner you've got to find the right one out of the nine. But, if you're laying, any one of the other eight will do it for you.'

'Sounds easy when you say it like that.'

'It is easier but a couple of winners in quick succession and you can be in deep trouble.'

'I see that,' said Dixon.

'There's a blanket ban on trainers laying their own horses and I'm not suggesting that Hesp has been doing that. But someone has been making a good deal of money laying his horses and they never win, as you know.'

'One did yesterday,' said Dixon.

'Really?'

'Yes. At Exeter. His first horse lost. Then I let him know we were there and, lo and behold, his second horse won.'

'Someone will have lost a lot of money on that, I expect,' said Spiers. 'You'll not be popular.'

'Tell me about these irregular betting patterns,' said Dixon.

'We monitor all betting live in real time from our HQ at Newmarket. We look for patterns that shouldn't be there. It's all in this file, which is a copy you can keep, but what we've seen is large lay bets on Hesp's horses and sometimes corresponding back bets on the joint or second favourite.'

'How large is large?' asked Jane.

'Sometimes up to five thousand pounds. They're clever, though. They know we'll be watching so they feed the money into the market over several hours. Occasionally one of Hesp's horses will run with nothing unusual about the betting at all.'

'And you don't think it's him.'

'No, there's someone behind him. He denied all knowledge of it, as I said on the phone.'

'And we can keep this file?'

'Yes, that's a copy for you.'

Dixon opened it.

'There's a copy of Hesp's interview transcript in there too,' said Spiers. 'Those are the betting spreadsheets.'

'Talk me through one of these entries then, so I know what's going on,' said Dixon.

'Sure. What you're looking at are the volumes, the money, matched up on the exchange at the different odds and the times too.'

'Matched up?'

'Yes. That's where someone places a back bet and it's matched with someone willing to lay it at those odds.'

'I see,' said Dixon.

'The odds will be changing the whole time, as you can see. Someone may place a back bet at odds of five to one and the layer may wait until another person tries to back at four to one before accepting it. It's like bidding, really. A financial market of sorts.'

'Bloody complicated,' said Dixon.

'It can be,' replied Spiers. 'There are software packages you can buy that will do it for you and hundreds of different systems out there for picking winners and losers. There are even laying tipsters.'

'When we were at Exeter yesterday, Hesp's groom phoned one of the on course bookies and he immediately changed the odds on Hesp's horse from two to one to four to one . . .'

'I expect he told the bookie the horse wouldn't be winning. He could safely increase his odds then and outbid the other on course bookies.'

'So, on the second of Hesp's horses, when he knew we were there, the groom phoned the bookie and this time he shortened the odds . . .'

'Because he knew the horse might win this time,' said Spiers.

'Then he went to the Bet29 website . . .'

'That would have been to back the horse himself at the highest odds he could find to limit his losses. What he pays out on the course is covered by what he wins on Bet29. It's hedging his bets.'

Dixon shook his head.

'There's a lot of money changing hands, Inspector, sometimes millions on a single race. That's why we take the integrity of the sport so seriously.'

'I can see that, Mr Spiers. Thank you, you've been very helpful.'

'What happens now?' asked Spiers.

'Well, I'm investigating the murder, as you know, but anything I find relevant to the betting side of things will be passed on to you, certainly,' replied Dixon.

'It'd be helpful to have a statement from you about yesterday at Exeter.'

'Yes, of course.'

—⁓—

Once out on the pavement, Dixon took out his phone and rang Louise Willmott.

'Louise, we're on our way now. We'll be back by 4.30 p.m. Pick up Hesp, Kevin Tanner and J Clapham Racing. Arrest them on suspicion of the murder of Noel Woodman and stick them in a cell until we get there. I'll ring DCI Lewis now and he'll rustle you up some help.'

—⁓—

They took a taxi and arrived at Paddington in time for the 1.03 p.m. train to Taunton.

'We'll get in about ten to three,' said Dixon.

'What about lunch?' asked Jane.

'There'll be a buffet car.'

They found an empty table and settled in for the journey, Dixon sitting with his back to the direction of travel and Jane sitting opposite him. She took the view that in a crash at one hundred plus miles an hour it really wouldn't matter which side of the table she was sitting on.

'What did you make of that?' asked Dixon.

'Complicated stuff,' replied Jane, 'but the bits that struck me were the sums of money involved and the fact Spiers thinks there's somebody behind Hesp.'

'Quite.'

'One thing's for sure. If it was this that Noel was going to blab about, then it's certainly motive enough to kill him.'

'It is. So, what about this somebody?'

'Could be anybody, couldn't it? A gambling syndicate, organised crime . . .'

'It's not gambling, though, is it? There's no gamble involved. It's cheating, pure and simple.'

'That leaves organised crime, then,' replied Jane.

Dixon looked out the window at the backs of the houses passing by as the train moved slowly west out of inner London. He reached into his trouser pocket and took out a coin.

'Heads or tails?'

'Tails,' said Jane.

Dixon flicked the coin into the air, caught it and laid it flat on the back of his left hand.

'Tails it is. Want anything from the buffet car?'

'Where is everybody, then, Louise?' asked Dixon.

'In the cells, Sir.'

'All suitably outraged, no doubt?'

'Mr Clapham was, but I got the impression the other two were expecting a visit from us.'

'Really?'

'Yes. Clapham and Hesp have requested a solicitor. They're on the way now.'

'Tanner first, then, I think. Then Clapham. We'll let Hesp sweat. Well done, Louise.'

Dixon and Jane were waiting in an interview room when Tanner was led in by a uniformed officer. He was small, much the same size as Noel and no doubt wanted to be a jockey some day, thought Dixon. He had short blonde hair and had clearly come straight from the stables. His jodhpurs were grubby and his Wellington boots covered in mud.

Dixon reminded Tanner that he was under arrest and cautioned him again for the tape.

'You have declined a solicitor. Is that right?'

'Yes.'

'How long have you worked for Michael Hesp?'

'About nine months.'

'So, you knew Noel well?'

'Ish.'

'Did you share the static caravan?'

'No. I stayed at home. I've moved into it now, though.'

'Five pounds an hour with free board and lodging?'

'Yes.'

'And no doubt the promise of one day being a jockey?'

Tanner nodded.

'Where were you on the morning he was killed?'

'At home. I left about 5 a.m. and got to the stables and found him. It's all in my statement.'

'And your parents can vouch for that, can they?'

'My mother can. My father's dead.'

'Where's home?'

'Bridgwater.'

'Did you see anything unusual on that morning?'

'No.'

'Tell me about the telephone call I saw you make to J Clapham Racing yesterday.'

The question caught Tanner off guard. He turned his head sharply and looked towards the door. Dixon waited. Tanner began picking at the seam of his jodhpurs with his left hand.

'Kevin, we have reason to believe that Noel was murdered because he was about to reveal some important information. At the moment that looks like it may have been a betting scam. It also looks to me as if you are involved in it.'

'It's not like that.'

'Tell me what it's like.'

Silence.

'From where I'm sitting you have a powerful motive for murder.'

'I didn't kill him.'

'But you know who did?'

'No.'

'Tell me about the betting scam.'

'I can't.'

'Why not?'

'I just can't.'

'Let me put it another way, then. We know about the betting scam, Kevin. One way or another, it's over. Kaput. At the very least, Hesp will lose his licence and you'll be out of a job. At worst, you'll be convicted of murder and do life.'

'I didn't kill him.'

Tanner began to panic. Dixon watched the beads of sweat forming on his forehead. He had pulled a thread from the seam of his jodhpurs and was tugging at it. Dixon waited.

'Noel was in on it.'

'What?'

'The betting scam.'

'Go on.'

'Michael gets the jockeys to hold the horses back. Make sure they don't win. Noel would tip Clapham off for a few quid each time.'

'And?'

'That's it. When Noel died, Clapham asked me if I'd do the same.'

'So, you're saying that Michael Hesp is deliberately holding his horses back?'

Silence.

'Let's hear it, Kevin.'

'Yes.'

'Why?'

'You know why.'

'We need to hear it from you.'

'They lay the horses on the betting exchanges . . .'

'Who do?'

'No way. That's it. I'm not saying any more.'

'Who, Kevin?'

'No comment.'

After several more 'no comments' from Tanner, Dixon terminated the interview at 4.25 p.m. Tanner was taken back to a cell in the custody suite. Dixon turned to Jane.

'If Noel was in on it, it's unlikely that he was going to go public with it, isn't it?'

'Still possible, I suppose, but unlikely,' replied Jane.

'And it seems to me Tanner and Clapham were just taking advantage of what was going on to make some small change on the side.'

'Looks like it.'

'You and Louise can interview Clapham. You know what to ask him?'

'I do.'

Dixon waited in his office while Jane and Louise interviewed Jeremy Clapham. He fetched himself a coffee from the machine and spent the time reading the British Horseracing Authority file that he had brought back from London. He now understood the terminology and the basic principles but some of the maths still eluded him. He had never been very good at maths, which is why he had trained as a lawyer rather than an accountant before joining the police.

He powered up his computer and checked his email. There was a telephone call from Jon Woodman at Exeter Prison, no doubt wanting to know what was going on, but otherwise nothing of interest. Jon would have to wait. Not least because Dixon wasn't at all sure that he had anything relevant to tell him, apart from the fact that his brother had been on the fiddle.

The interview with Clapham lasted no more than thirty minutes.

'He's a complete shit,' said Jane.

'We meet quite a few of those in this line of work,' said Dixon.

'It probably didn't help that we pulled him out of the Betting Ring at Wincanton,' said Louise.

'My heart bleeds,' replied Dixon. 'What did he have to say for himself?'

'Denials, mostly,' said Jane. 'He denied murdering Noel, but then we don't really think he did, do we?'

'No.'

'He completely denied knowing Noel or Tanner, too, but backtracked when we talked about mobile phone records. Then he said he knew them and spoke to them both from time to time, but not about racing.'

'What did he say about yesterday?'

'He said he did speak to Tanner but the change of odds was pure coincidence, prompted by checking the betting exchanges after each call.'

'He must think we're bloody stupid.'

'I got the impression that's exactly what he thought, Sir,' said Louise.

'OK, rearrest them for obtaining a pecuniary advantage by deception and then release them both on bail. Then we'll have a word with Mr Hesp.'

— ⌣ —

The interview with Michael Hesp proved to be something of an anticlimax. It lasted no more than ten minutes, Hesp answering 'no comment' to each and every question asked of him. Dixon pressed him on the events of the previous day at Exeter and also the British Horseracing Authority investigation, all to no avail. The only occasion Dixon thought he had made any impression on Hesp was when he asked him about the 'money' behind the betting scam. Dixon thought he recognised a fleeting look of fear in Hesp's eyes, but he soon recovered his composure and reverted to 'no comment' answers.

Dixon brought the interview to a close just after 5.30 p.m. Hesp was rearrested for the deception offence and then released on bail.

'What did you make of that, Jane?'

'He's shitting himself.'

'He is, but he did a good job of covering it up.'

'Who was his solicitor, Louise? I've not seen him before.'

'Paul Richards from Bristol.'

'Bristol?'

'Yes.'

'He came all the way from Bristol for that?'

'Yes, Sir.'

'Find out what you can about Richards, will you, Jane? You can head off, Louise. We'll see you back here in the morning.'

'Thank you, Sir.'

— ⌣ —

Dixon and Jane were back at his cottage in Brent Knoll by 6.15 p.m. Dixon took Monty for a walk while Jane put a frozen fish pie in the oven. Then they opened a bottle of red wine and sat on the sofa. It had been a tiring day and it wasn't long before Dixon was asleep. He woke up briefly for his supper before falling asleep again. Soap operas tended to have that effect on him.

The next thing he knew it was 2 a.m. He was in bed, but was not entirely sure how he had got there. Jane was asleep next to him and Monty was curled up on the end of the bed by his feet. Monty had his own bed on the floor, next to Dixon, but rarely slept in it.

Dixon lay in bed dozing, his mind wandering from the sea cliffs at Pembroke to the slate quarries of North Wales. Then to a bunker on Burnham and Berrow golf course with a severed head in it.

Suddenly, he couldn't breathe. He opened his eyes. Monty was standing on his chest, staring at him, his head tipped to one side. The dog turned and ran to the end of the bed. Dixon watched as he stood there, growling softly at the curtains, much as he had done only three nights before when PC Cole had arrived in the early hours.

Dixon sat up. He could hear footsteps in the road outside. He climbed out of bed and looked out of the crack between the curtains. He could see two men, one carrying a double barrelled shotgun and the other a large blade. It glinted in the street lights. Both were wearing balaclavas. Further along Brent Street was a car. Engine on, lights off.

Dixon woke Jane. He put his hand over her mouth to keep her quiet.

'What is it?' she whispered.

'We've got company. Call it in. We need armed response. One of them's got a gun.'

'Oh, shit.' Jane started to shake.

Her phone was on the bedside table.

'Don't panic, Jane. Just make the call. And keep hold of Monty. If they get past me, let him go.'

Jane hooked her fingers in Monty's collar with one hand and dialled 999 with the other.

Dixon opened the divan drawer under his side of the bed. He felt down through the socks and underwear until his fingers closed around the handle of his great grandfather's trench cosh. It was a bamboo cane with a lump of lead on the end, all wrapped in brown leather. He put his right hand through the loop and gripped the handle as tight as he could.

Then he reached down behind his bedside table with his left hand and produced an ice axe. His last souvenir from his old climbing days, it had seen him safely to the top of Mont Blanc and back down again. He had kept it for just such an occasion as this. He held the top of the axe in his left hand with the handle running along the outside of his left forearm.

'Be careful,' said Jane.

Dixon closed the bedroom door and crept down the stairs. He could hear Jane on the phone. There was an urgency in her voice. Dixon was relieved that she had got through. Help would be on its way soon. But soon enough?

He reached the bottom of the stairs before he heard the back door creaking. Then the plastic splitting, which told him that it was being levered open with a crow bar. He ran over to the kitchen doorway and looked in. He could see two shadows outside through the frosted glass. One was trying to open the door. The other was standing behind him.

He could hear the car parked further along Brent Street, its engine still running. That meant a third man. The getaway driver. Either way, he'd scarper, with or without his passengers.

Dixon stepped back into the shadows under the stairs and waited. His heart was racing. He began to shake and tried to focus on regulating his breathing. He knew this was going to end in one of two ways.

Finally, the back door gave way. Dixon felt the cold night air rush into the cottage. It was only then that he realised he was dressed in just his underpants. He shook his head. No good worrying about it now.

He heard footsteps on the kitchen floor. First one set then another. Both men were in the kitchen. Dixon waited, hidden in the shadows.

Voices. Whispering. He couldn't hear what was being said.

The barrels of the shotgun appeared in the doorway, edging forward. It was sawn off. Perfect for close range work. Then gloved hands came into view as the intruder edged further into the living room. He was right handed, with his left hand holding the stock.

Dixon waited, still hidden in the shadows. He took a deep breath, silently through his nose, and counted to three. Then he swung the trench cosh as hard as he could at the gloved hand holding the shotgun. Dixon felt the vibration of the cosh hitting wrist bone coursing through the bamboo handle. The soft crunching of the bone was followed by a loud scream. Both barrels of the gun went off, hitting Dixon's TV and DVD collection, before the gun fell to the floor.

Monty started barking. He had broken away from Jane and was scrabbling at the inside of the bedroom door.

Dixon darted forward. The man was still screaming, his right hand hanging at right angles from his arm. Dixon allowed the trench cosh to slip from his grasp and picked up the shotgun in his right hand, holding it by the barrels. Then he swung it like a tennis racket at the head of the intruder. The gun butt hit the man on the left side of his forehead. The screaming stopped and he dropped to the floor.

Silence.

Dixon looked up and stepped back. The second man ran forward, his right arm raised above his head. Dixon could see the blade of a machete glinting in the moonlight that was streaming in through the kitchen windows. The man jumped the lifeless body lying on the floor and swung the machete at Dixon's head. Dixon raised his left arm to deflect the blow. A searing pain tore through his left shoulder. He felt the blade bite deep into the rubber handle of his ice axe before hitting the steel underneath.

The man was off balance. Dixon took his chance. He swung the shotgun again as hard as he could, another forearm smash that would have been the envy of any tennis player. He connected with the left side of the man's head. He heard a crack. Was it the shotgun butt or the man's skull splitting? He hoped, prayed, it was skull.

Silence.

The man fell backwards, almost in slow motion, landing in a crumpled heap behind the front door of the cottage. He pulled the door curtain off the wall as he fell and it came down on top of him.

Dixon could hear sirens in the distance. Monty was still barking.

Dixon ran outside, still in his underpants, just in time to see a red estate car speeding away. It raced to the end of Brent Street and turned right. He didn't get the number plate.

The sirens were getting louder. Dixon ran back into the cottage. Neither intruder was stirring.

'It's all right, Jane, you can come out now.'

The bedroom door flew open and Jane ran down the stairs behind Monty. She threw her arms around Dixon, while Monty sniffed the bodies lying on the floor.

'There was a third one in a car but he hooked it,' said Dixon. He was still holding the shotgun in his right hand and the ice axe in his left. The trench cosh was dangling from his right wrist on the loop.

'Are they dead?' asked Jane.

'Who gives a . . . ?'

There was a knock at the front door.

'Are you all right in there?'

'Who is it?' shouted Dixon.

'Rob from the Red Cow.'

'Fine, thanks, Rob. You'd better go home. Keep your doors locked and don't open them for anyone.'

'What's happened?'

'I'll tell you tomorrow.'

'OK. As long as you're all right.'

'Fine, thanks, really.'

The sirens were getting louder. Dixon could hear the helicopter overhead.

He handed the shotgun to Jane.

'I'm going to put some clothes on. If they move, hit 'em again.'

'You're going to need an ambulance,' said Jane. 'Look.'

Dixon looked at his left shoulder. Blood had soaked through the dressing and was running down the left side of his chest.

'I'm more concerned about my bloody telly. Look at that,' he said, pointing at it with the trench cosh. 'It was practically brand new.'

The television had taken the full force of both barrels. The screen had shattered and bits of glass were lying everywhere.

'My DVDs have gone too . . .'

'Every cloud . . .' said Jane.

They started to laugh. A nervous laugh at first, then they hugged each other tightly. Jane began to sob.

'It's the relief, I think,' said Jane.

'It is.'

Suddenly, blue lights were all around them, reflecting on the walls and ceiling of the cottage.

'Trousers,' said Dixon, running up the stairs. He reappeared a few seconds later pulling on a pair of jeans at the top of the stairs.

'Armed police.' The shout came from outside.

'Safe. 3275 Inspector Dixon. I have the gun. We need an ambulance. Two intruders on the ground.'

Dixon put Monty on his lead just as an armed police officer appeared at the back door. Jane held up the shotgun, still holding it by the barrels.

'This is Detective Constable Jane Winter,' said Dixon.

'Safe,' shouted the officer. 'An ambulance is on its way, Sir. It'll be here in five minutes.'

Chapter Six

A red estate car heading towards East Brent. Get the helicopter after it, will you?'

'Yes, Sir. Chief Inspector Bateman's on his way.'

'Oh, joy,' said Dixon.

He was standing in the living room of his cottage, surveying what was left of his television. A paramedic was peeling the dressing off his left shoulder.

'You'll need to go to hospital for this, I'm afraid. You've torn the stitches.'

'Can't you just patch me up for the time being? Jane can drive me over when we've sorted this mess out.'

'Be sure that you do, though.'

'I will,' said Jane. She was sitting on the sofa watching four other paramedics working on the two intruders, both men still lying unconscious on the floor of Dixon's cottage. The man who had been armed with the shotgun was being moved onto a stretcher, his neck in a brace and his right forearm in a splint.

'Are they . . . ?'

'They're both alive. We'll take them to Weston for further examination.'

'Right,' said Jane.

PC Cole appeared in the kitchen doorway.

'You all right, Sir?'

'We're OK, thank you, Cole.'

'I've bagged up the gun, machete and crow bar. I just need your ice axe and cosh, if you don't mind, Sir,' said Cole.

Dixon looked down. He was still holding the trench cosh in his right hand and the ice axe in his left. He slipped his hand out of the loop on the cosh and then handed both to Cole.

'Look after them, will you? I want them back.'

'Yes, Sir. I've got orders to go with these two to the hospital,' said Cole, gesturing towards to the two men on the floor. 'Mr Bateman's here and DCI Lewis is on his way, as well, apparently.'

'We are privileged, Jane,' said Dixon.

The paramedics carried the first of the two stretchers out through the back door.

'You insured, Sir?' asked Cole.

'Yes,' replied Dixon.

'A nice new telly, then . . .'

'Let me through, will you, Constable,' said Bateman.

Cole moved to one side, allowing Chief Inspector Bateman to step into the room.

'What is it with you, Dixon? You seem to attract trouble like flies round a turd.'

'I'd prefer moths round a light, Sir, if you don't mind.'

Bateman smiled.

'And you don't think you used excessive force?'

'No, I don't.'

'Neither do I. Well done.'

'Thank you, Sir.'

'The CPS and Independent Complaints may want to look at it, though. You know what they're like.'

'Two men break into my house in the dead of night, armed with a shotgun and a machete. If I'd had a gun I'd have shot 'em, Sir, and it still wouldn't have been excessive force.'

'Quite.'

'He should get a medal, Sir,' said Jane.

'Monty should get that. God alone knows what would've happened if he hadn't woken me up.'

The remaining paramedics stood up, ready to carry the other stretcher out through the back door. They had removed the man's balaclava and paused briefly so Dixon could see his face. The man had a three inch gash above his left eye that looked through to the bone. He was dressed from head to toe in black. His mouth and nose were covered by an oxygen mask.

'What do you think, Jane? Thirtyish?'

'About that.'

'Eastern European?'

'Possibly.'

'All right, take him away,' said Bateman.

Dixon could hear the helicopter overhead again.

'They lost the car, I suppose?'

'Never picked it up,' said Bateman.

Dixon shook his head. He walked over and looked at what was left of his DVD collection. He picked up a box and opened it. Shards of broken DVD fell to the floor.

'Goodbye, Mr Chips,' he muttered.

'Nothing that can't be replaced,' said Jane.

'You all right?' The voice came from the kitchen. Dixon looked over. It was DCI Lewis.

'Fine, Sir, thank you.'

'You've rattled the wrong cage, this time.'

'Or the right one?'

'SOCO will be here in a minute, so get some clothes on and let's get you out of here.'

'Where . . . ?'

'Hospital would be a good starting point, by the looks of things,' said Lewis.

Blood had started to drip down the left side of Dixon's chest again.

'I'll take Monty to my parents' and meet you there,' said Jane.

'SOCO can secure the back door when they've finished, if you're not back by then.'

Dixon heard the back doors of the ambulance being slammed shut in the road outside and looked through the front window to see it leaving, with PC Cole following in a patrol car. Then he went upstairs, got dressed and followed DCI Lewis and Jane out into the road.

Brent Street had been sealed off at both ends and blue lights were still flashing all around, lighting up the cottages and the pub. Most had lights on in the windows and uniformed officers were going from house to house, telling residents to stay indoors.

Dixon was not going to be popular with his neighbours.

It was just after 6 a.m. by the time Jane arrived at Weston Hospital. Dixon was in a private room, sitting sideways on the bed with his legs dangling over the side.

'What's happening?'

'They want the surgeon who operated on it to have a look, so I'm stuck here until he gets his arse out of bed.'

'And Lewis?'

'He left ages ago,' replied Dixon. 'How's Monty?'

'Fine. My parents' cat wasn't too chuffed about it, though. Fancy a cup of tea?'

'They told me not to have anything in case they have to operate again.'

'What about your blood sugar?'

'They took it an hour or so ago and it was fine.'

'Any news on our house guests?'

'No.'

There was a knock at the door.

'Come in,' shouted Dixon.

'I'm looking for Detective Inspector Dixon.'

'That'll be me.'

'I'm DCS Collyer, Head of Operations, Bristol Zephyr team.'

They shook hands and Dixon introduced Jane. DCS Collyer looked the part in a smart grey suit, white shirt and red tie. He had short dark hair, a moustache and wore spectacles.

'Zephyr means organised crime, and a detective chief superintendent, too, Sir. What've we done to deserve that?' asked Dixon.

'You've had quite a night of it, I gather,' said Collyer.

'You could say that,' replied Jane.

'It's a good thing they were only trying to scare you . . .'

'Scare us?'

'Yes, if they'd wanted you dead, you'd be at the bottom of the Bristol Channel by now.'

'Who is this 'they', then, Sir?' asked Dixon.

'Your two visitors are Besim Raslan and Ardita Besmir.'

'What . . . ?'

'Albanian.'

'Albanian?'

'That's right. Serious people. They're part of a gang that operates out of a bookmakers shop in Whiteladies Road. It's just a front, of course.'

'Of course.'

'They're into drugs, mainly, and a bit of gambling on the side. We've been watching them for some time.'

'Are they going to be all right?'

'Who?'

'The two . . .'

'Oh, yes, fine, I think. One has had an op on a badly broken arm and got away with a bad headache, the other needed surgery for a bleed on the brain. He should be all right, though.'

'Where are they now?'

'One's on a ward and the other's in intensive care. Under guard. They'll be remanded in custody, do ten to fifteen and then be deported, I expect.'

'Gits.'

'You must have trodden on some toes to merit a visit. What are you investigating?'

'What've you been told, Sir?'

'About a murder at Gidley's Racing Stables near Bridgwater . . .'

'The victim was about to blow the whistle on something big and we've been looking into the possibility that this 'something big' was a betting scam. The British Horseracing Authority believe that the trainer's been holding his horses back so that others, presumably this lot from Whiteladies Road, could lay them on the betting exchanges. The trainer denied it, of course, but the other groom at the yard admitted it. Both looked scared shitless when I pressed them on who was behind it. They had a winner on Thursday, though.'

'A winner? That will have lost the Albanians a lot of money.'

'You sound like you know about this betting scam?'

'I do.'

'I'm not convinced it's the motive for the murder, though, because the victim was actively skimming on the side.'

'Involved in it, you mean?'

'Yes. And using the information to make a few quid extra for himself.'

'Interesting.'

'It is, Sir, and given what you've just told me, I'm even more convinced that it's not the motive.'

'Why?'

'If it was, our victim would be at the bottom of the Bristol Channel now, wouldn't he?'

'He'd have just disappeared?' asked Jane.

'He would. Quietly, no fuss. And with Noel, who'd have thought anything odd about that?'

'True.'

'You mentioned the gang was into drugs too, Sir?' asked Dixon.

'Yes. We think they've been bringing it into the country using the horse lorries. Cocaine, primarily. They go backwards and for-wards across the Channel on the ferry to Brittany. There's a farm over there where some of the horses rest, apparently. At least, that's the pretext. They take some horses over and bring others back so it doesn't look suspicious.'

'And no one's found anything?'

'No, the Border lot have been over the lorries, with dogs too, and found nothing,' replied Collyer. 'We've tried to get someone on the inside, but no luck yet.'

'So, you've been watching the yard?' asked Dixon.

'On and off.'

'Why weren't we told?'

'We didn't think . . .'

'Well, I bloody well did need to know . . .' Dixon shook his head. 'I think we can rule that out as the motive anyway.'

'Why?' asked Jane.

'Same reason. If Noel was threatening to blab about it, one telephone call and he'd have just disappeared. I bet he knew it, too.'

'Tanner seemed to,' replied Jane.

'That he did. And Hesp,' said Dixon. 'I wonder how much Mrs Harcourt knows about all this.'

'We've been working on the basis that she's a reluctant participant,' said Collyer. 'If she does know, she's not happy about it.'

'How do you know that?'

'We listen.'

'What does that m . . . ?' asked Jane.

'Don't ask,' said Dixon.

'What was your victim going to sing about, then?' asked Collyer.

'Time for a closer look at his private life, I think.'

'Well, keep me posted if you turn up anything I need to know.'

'Yes, Sir.'

'And look after yourself.'

'Thank you, Sir.'

'And if you fancy a change, let me know. We can always make room for good people in the Zephyr Team.'

'Didn't think. Didn't bloody think. People trot that out as if it somehow makes it all right,' said Dixon.

'They do.'

'I'd rather they'd thought about it and decided not to tell me but "didn't bloody think" . . .'

'Calm down.'

'Idiots.'

Jane was driving Dixon's Land Rover.

'Can we get Monty first?'

Jane looked at her watch. It was nearly 10 a.m.

'Yes, fine.'

Dixon had been discharged from hospital, having not needed further surgery. The wound had been dressed, his arm was back in a sling and he had been prescribed more Tramadol. He leaned against the door pillar on the passenger side of the car and closed his eyes. Seconds later he was asleep.

He woke up when Jane pulled up outside his cottage.

'Where's . . . ?'

'In the back.'

Dixon looked over his shoulder to find Monty sitting on the floor behind him. Then he looked along Brent Street, which was now open. He could see three patrol cars parked at various points and police officers conducting house to house enquiries. The Scientific Services vans had gone so he would be allowed back into his cottage. Jane reversed into the drive at the side and then parked behind the cottage.

The back door had been screwed shut from the inside to secure it.

'We'll need to use the front door,' said Dixon.

They stood in the doorway looking at the wreckage of the television and DVDs.

'Are those pellet holes in the wall behind the telly?' asked Jane.

'A bit of Polyfilla will soon sort that out.'

The door curtain had been rolled up and thrown on the sofa. Dixon noticed two patches of blood on the carpet where the Albanians had lain unconscious, bleeding from their head wounds.

'You got a carpet shampooer I can borrow?'

'No. Won't your insurers sort that out?'

'I'll ring them.'

'Right. Well, I'll leave you to it.'

'Where are you off to?'

'It's my dad's birthday. Out to lunch. Remember?'

'No.'

'I'll be back fourish.' She kissed Dixon and then left in his Land Rover.

Dixon rang his insurance company and then began tidying up. Not an easy task one handed. He threw the door curtain under the stairs. Then he shut Monty in the kitchen to keep him out of the way and picked up the large pieces of glass from the television screen one by one, putting them in an empty cardboard box with the broken DVDs. The only one to have survived the shotgun blast was *The Dambusters*. Next he hoovered up the smaller bits of glass, before dumping the lot outside the back door.

He sat down with a cup of tea. Monty jumped up and sat on his lap.

'What are we going to do, then, matey?'

Dixon sat staring into space. He thought about Noel. He was making money out of the betting scam and wouldn't have dared blow the whistle on the drug dealing, either. So, it must have been something personal to him. He was a rent boy, of course, which presented him with plenty of opportunity for blackmail. Dixon felt a sense of direction returning to the enquiry.

Then he heard a noise outside. He jumped up and ran into the kitchen for a knife. Monty started barking. Dixon waited out of sight. A figure appeared in the small frosted glass window in the front door. Two letters were pushed through the letterbox and dropped onto the mat.

'For fuck's sake,' muttered Dixon.

He picked up the letters and threw them on the side in the kitchen. Then he fetched his laptop, navigated to Google and searched for free horse race laying systems. He spent the next ten minutes scrolling through the results, clicking on various links, before downloading a copy of *Betting Exchange Bookie*, which the author described as a foolproof horse race laying system.

Dixon read the short PDF file in twenty minutes, making various notes as he did so. When he was finished, he had a list of rules for selecting a losing horse. He read aloud.

'The race must have at least nine runners. Never lay a horse that won its last race. There must be at least two other runners with a Racing Post Rating within five of your selection. Your selection should not be the only horse carrying top weight. Never lay unless the odds have drifted out by more than two points. Never lay at odds over eight to one.'

He went to the *Racing Post* website and looked at the racecards for the day. Lingfield, Wincanton, Naas and Ascot.

'Let's have a bit of fun, shall we, old chap,' he said, looking at Monty.

He navigated to Bet29 and signed up. Then he reached for his wallet and deposited one hundred pounds.

Racing got under way at 12.30 p.m. but it was the 1.05 p.m. at Wincanton before he found a suitable candidate. Napoleon. He came fourth last time out and had started the day at odds of five to one but drifted out to seven to one by 1 p.m., just before the off. He was not top weight and there were two other competitive horses in the race, according to the Racing Post Ratings.

Dixon layed him for ten pounds at odds of seven to one and waited for the bet to be matched. He began to sweat. If Napoleon lost, Dixon would win ten pounds. If the horse won the race, he would have to pay out seventy pounds. He could feel his resolve draining away. Seventy quid? He was about to click 'Cancel' when the bet was matched. Too late to back out now.

Dixon would not be able to watch the race on the television and would have to be content with watching the odds change as the race progressed. If Napoleon was doing well, the odds would shorten; if not, they would drift out still further. Dixon watched and waited. Suddenly, the betting screen froze and then went blank, before appearing again with the words 'In Play' across the middle. The race was under way.

When the 'In Play' odds appeared, Napoleon had shortened in to evens. He must be near the front, thought Dixon. He watched the odds of the other horses. They were bouncing around all over the place and he decided he could read nothing into that. He could feel his heart beating in his chest.

Then he noticed that Napoleon's odds had drifted out to six to one. Another horse was in at odds of one to two. That's odds on, thought Dixon. He must be going to win. He looked back to Napoleon at odds of fifteen to one, then fifty to one. Dixon relaxed. Napoleon had lost.

'Easy money,' he said, scratching Monty behind the ears. 'Let's try another.'

He scanned the racecards for the next few races. Nothing at Naas, except a short priced favourite against very weak opposition. Flat racing on the all weather track at Lingfield got under way at 1.20 p.m. but the first race had an odds on favourite. The second favourite looked interesting but the odds were shortening rather than drifting. Lots of people were backing him and there was probably a good reason for that. Dixon moved onto the next race.

Ascot and the 1.30 p.m. He looked down the betting screen and found Spilt Milk, second favourite but with odds that had drifted from three to one to five to one. Dixon checked the form. Spilt Milk was not top weight and had not won her last race. She looked perfect.

Five to one would cost Dixon fifty pounds if she won. He laid the horse at odds of five to one and waited for the bet to be matched up. The odds continued to drift out until his bet was matched. He waited.

As before, the screen froze and then the 'In Play' message was displayed. Dixon watched the odds bouncing around, trying not to get too agitated. Spilt Milk's odds drifted out to seventeen to one and then still further to one hundred to one and beyond. She must have been well off the pace almost from the off.

'I'm in the wrong business, Monty,' said Dixon.

Prince Billy in the 1.35 p.m. at Wincanton caught Dixon's eye for the wrong reason. He scanned the form and read aloud.

'Jockey S McCarthy, Trainer M Hesp.'

Tempting. He checked the odds. They were drifting, which meant the horse was not expected to win, but then he knew that. Dixon noticed that more money had been matched up on Prince Billy than on any other horse in the race, including the favourite. The irregular betting pattern again.

Dixon entered ten pounds in the laying column and selected the odds. His mouse hovered over the 'Submit' button.

'No, Monty, cheats never prosper.'

Dixon hit the 'Back' button and watched the race unfold without placing a bet. Almost immediately the odds on the favourite in the race went straight out to one thousand to one. Dixon thought he must have fallen or pulled up. Prince Billy's odds shortened and kept getting shorter. Dixon smiled. Prince Billy was doing well. Either Hesp had told the jockey not to hold him back or his plan was scuppered by the favourite falling.

Dixon withdrew all his money back to his credit card and logged out. Then he closed his laptop and put it away.

'My father always told me to quit while you're ahead, old son,' he said, scratching Monty behind the ears. Dixon had got what he wanted. A clear understanding of the mechanics of backing and laying horses on the betting exchanges.

'Besides, matey, it's a mug's game.'

He opened a can of beer and took two Tramadol. Then he fell asleep on the sofa with Monty curled up beside him.

Jane arrived back just as it was getting dark and parked behind the cottage, as usual. She thought it odd that all the lights were off. She tried the back door, before remembering that it had been secured from the inside, and then walked around to the front door. She peered through the frosted glass and could see no sign of life. There was no barking, either. That could mean only one thing.

She walked over to the Red Cow and found Dixon asleep in the corner of the lounge bar. Monty was lying on the floor at his feet, awake and alert.

'I didn't like to wake him,' said Rob. 'Sounds like you had a hell of a night.'

'We did.'

'What can I get you?'

'Gin and tonic, please,' replied Jane. 'How many's he had?'

'That's his second.'

Jane looked at the pint glass on the table in front of Dixon. It was half empty.

'Must be the painkillers.'

She reached into her handbag for her purse.

'On the house,' said Rob.

'Thank you.'

Jane sat opposite Dixon and tapped his foot under the table. He woke up.

'What time is it?'

'Fiveish.'

He rubbed his eyes.

'How long have you been in here?' asked Jane.

'About an hour, I suppose.'

'You all right?'

'Felt a bit of a sitting duck in the cottage . . .'

Jane took a large swig of gin and tonic.

'Drink up. We'll go and stay at my flat. It's got a telly, for a start.'

'Great. I'll bring what's left of my DVD coll . . .'

'Don't even think about it.'

Chapter Seven

The CID Room at Bridgwater Police Station was a hive of activity, despite the fact that it was first thing Sunday morning. Dixon and Jane arrived to find DI Janice Courtenay briefing her team on an aggravated burglary the night before near Westonzoyland. DCI Lewis was listening in. At the far end of the room, Dave Harding and Mark Pearce were finishing off the paperwork on Dixon's previous case for submission to the CPS on Monday.

'All hail the conquering hero.'

'Piss off, Janice,' said Dixon, smiling.

Jane sat at her desk and switched on her computer. Dixon went into his office, closely followed by DCI Lewis.

'You had a visit from Peter Collyer?'

'They knew, they bloody well knew what was going on at that yard and . . .'

Dixon stopped mid-sentence. He was looking past DCI Lewis at the vending machine against the far wall of the CID Room. Feeding coins into it was DS Harry Unwin.

Dixon brushed past DCI Lewis and marched across the room, knocking a pile of papers off the corner of Jane's desk as he went past. Harry Unwin heard the noise and turned to see Dixon steaming towards him. Unwin tried to back away but there was nowhere for him to go. As he closed in, Dixon reached up with his right hand and pinned Unwin to the front of the vending machine by the throat.

Dixon glared at Unwin.

'I tried to warn you . . .' said Unwin.

Dixon spoke through gritted teeth. 'Was that before or after you gave them my address?'

'Dixon! Put him down!' shouted Lewis.

Jane arrived and tried to release Unwin from Dixon's hand.

'In my office now. Both of you.'

Dixon released Unwin and turned to follow DCI Lewis into his office. Unwin straightened his jacket and tie and then followed them.

Lewis slammed the door behind them.

'What the bloody hell do you think you're playing at?'

The question was addressed to Dixon. He remained silent.

'I appreciate that you've been through a lot in the last day or so . . .'

'It's fine, Sir, really,' said Unwin.

'You won't be making a formal complaint?'

'No, Sir.'

'Well, I'm sure Inspector Dixon is grateful. Thank you, Harry, you may go.'

Harry Unwin left the room.

'That prick told them where I live.'

'Of course he did. But it's in hand. That's all I can tell you. Is that clear?'

Dixon nodded.

'Go home and get some rest.'

'Yes, Sir.'

'And another thing.'

Dixon turned back to face Lewis.

'You've got him by the throat with your right and your left's in a sling.'

'Yes.'

'What were you going to hit him with?'

'That is not something to which I had applied my mind, Sir.'

Lewis smiled.

'Get out of my sight.'

———

'C'mon, Jane, let's get out of here.'

'Where are we going?'

'Spaxton.'

They walked out to Dixon's Land Rover in silence and were heading west out of Bridgwater on Durleigh Road before Jane spoke.

'What was that all about?'

'Unwin gave the Albanians my address.'

'Harry?'

'Yes.'

'Couldn't they have got it off the electoral roll?'

'I'm not on it yet.'

'Directory enquiries?'

'No landline.'

'Are you sure?'

'Yes.'

'What did Lewis have to say?'

'He told me to get some rest.'

'So, we're going to Spaxton?'

'Briefly. Then maybe lunch somewhere and a walk on the beach?' asked Dixon.

'Sounds good to me,' replied Jane.

It was a sunny autumn day with a clear blue sky and not a breath of wind. They forked right at the eastern end of Durleigh Reservoir onto Spaxton Road. Dixon watched the dinghies sailing up and down as they drove past.

They left the Land Rover in the small car park at Gidley's Racing Stables. Both horse lorries were sitting off to the left of the entrance, as they had been before. The larger of the two was black with gold lettering, 'Michael Hesp Racing, Spaxton, Somerset'. The ramp at the back was open but the lorry was empty. Dixon walked up the ramp and looked around inside.

It had partitioning in place for up to six horses, but there were only three hay nets hanging from the rings on the wall. The floor was covered in muck and wood shavings. Underneath that was rubber matting. Beyond the stalls, a narrow corridor led through to a small living area with a sink, lavatory and dinette seating. The lorry was a little rough around the edges but otherwise clean and in good condition. A pile of dirty riding silks and jodhpurs had been left on the seat.

There was a small tack cabinet bolted to the wall. It was open, so Dixon looked inside. There were several bridles hanging on hooks on the inside of the door. Dixon could see two pairs of riding boots at the bottom and four horse racing saddles on racks, one above the other.

'Can I help you?'

The shout came from the rear of the lorry. Dixon walked back along the narrow corridor and down the ramp.

'You had another winner yesterday, Mr Hesp. Your luck must be changing.'

'Are you here for anything in particular or just snooping?'

'Investigating a murder, Mr Hesp. It's not all about your grubby little betting scam.'

'How dare you? I . . .'

'A 2007 six horse Iveco lorry with living space. What's that worth, then?'

'Well, I . . .'

'I can Google it . . .'

'About sixty thousand.'

'Really? And how do you afford that?'

'I paid for it with an inheritance.'

'Don't tell me, an elderly aunt?'

'Yes, actually.'

'And the Renault lorry over there. What about that?'

'That belongs to Georgina.'

'What's in the box on the roof?'

'Tack.'

'May I see?'

Hesp climbed up onto the roof of the lorry using the ladder bolted to the side. He opened the side of the fibreglass box on the roof to reveal several black leather and synthetic saddles.

'Just spares and other stuff.'

'That's fine, thank you, Mr Hesp.'

Hesp climbed down the ladder as Dixon walked towards his Land Rover.

'When does Westbrook Warrior race again?'

'Wednesday at Taunton.'

'Really? I may come and watch.'

It was getting dark as Dixon and Jane walked back along the beach towards the Pavilion. Sunday lunch at the Red Cow had been followed by a long walk out as far as the lighthouse and back. They had parked on the seafront near the Clarence and thought they might pop in for a drink before heading back to Jane's flat.

'Do you think we'll be welcome?' asked Jane.

'We'll soon find out.'

Their last visit to the Clarence had not ended well.

Dixon walked up the flight of concrete steps and waited at the top. Jane was still on the beach, rummaging in her pockets for the scented dog bags so she could pick up after Monty. Having an arm in a sling had some advantages, thought Dixon.

Suddenly, he heard soft footsteps behind him. He turned. Too late. He felt something dig into the right side of his back under his ribcage. He looked over his right shoulder and could see a gloved hand pressing the barrel of a gun into him. The man was small, dressed in black and wearing dark sunglasses. He had a moustache and dark stubble.

He nodded to the right.

'Get in the car.'

A strong eastern European accent.

Dixon looked over to see a large black Range Rover with tinted windows. The nearside passenger doors, front and back, were open. Dixon looked down the steps. Jane was at the bottom holding Monty on the lead. She looked up at him with panic in her eyes. He shook his head. Jane got the message and turned back towards the beach, soon hidden behind the sea wall.

Dixon walked over and got in the back of the Range Rover. The man slammed the door and then climbed into the front seat. The car sped off heading north along the Esplanade. They were speeding out of Burnham towards the motorway roundabout before the man sitting next to Dixon spoke.

'You are becoming a pain in the neck, as you English say, Mr Dixon.'

'And what do I call you? Mr Green? Colonel Mustard?'

'You may call me Zavan.'

Zavan was in his early sixties with grey hair and matching beard. He clearly stuck to the dress code for Albanian gangsters, wearing trousers, polo neck sweater and a sports jacket. All black. He spoke slowly and with a strong eastern European accent.

'And what do your friends call you?' asked Dixon.

'I have no friends.'

'You owe me a new television.'

'And you owe me two men. So we are quits, I think.'

Zavan turned in his seat to face Dixon and looked him up and down.

'What happened to your arm?'

'I got stabbed a week or so ago.'

'I read about that.'

The driver of the Range Rover spoke in Albanian. Zavan translated for Dixon.

'He said you dealt with Besim and Ardita with one arm. He would like to have seen that.'

'An Englishman's home is his castle . . .' replied Dixon.

Zavan threw his head back and roared with laughter. He stopped abruptly.

'You don't scare easy, do you, Mr Dixon?'

'No.'

'You are not scared now?'

'I'm working on the basis that if you wanted me dead I'd be at the bottom of the Bristol Channel . . .'

'We could be on our way there now,' said Zavan.

'We could. But then you wouldn't be here getting your hands dirty and I certainly wouldn't have been taken in broad daylight, now, would I?'

Zavan nodded. He spoke in Albanian to the driver. The Range Rover turned north on the A38 towards Bristol.

'We do not kill policemen, Mr Dixon. We are not barbarians.'

'And you're not stupid either.'

'That is true. We are not stupid.'

'So, what do you want?'

'Our interests do not conflict, yours and mine. You seek a murderer and we have killed no one.'

'But you are breaking the law,' replied Dixon.

'Mere trifles, by comparison,' said Zavan. 'Is that the right expression?'

'It is.'

'And they are someone else's problem, are they not?'

'They are.'

'We did not kill the groom. I give you my word.'

'And you don't know who did, I suppose.'

'No.'

'Hesp will be closed down. You know that?'

'The horse racing was never going to last long. And it was small change.'

Dixon decided not to let on that he knew about the drugs.

'And what about Hesp?'

'He will be more careful who he borrows money from next time,' replied Zavan.

'He'll have plenty of time to think about it.'

'So, we have an agreement?' asked Zavan.

'We have arrived at an understanding,' replied Dixon.

'Is there a difference?'

'There is. Buy yourself a dictionary.'

Zavan smiled and barked an order in Albanian. The Range Rover came to an abrupt halt on the side of the road.

'Goodbye, Mr Dixon. I hope our interests never conflict.'

'So do I.'

Dixon watched the Range Rover speed off towards Bristol, its lights disappearing into the distance. He looked around. He could see the lights of the Sidcot Arms set back from the road about five hundred yards away and started walking towards it. He reached into his pocket and rang Jane as he walked.

'Are you all right? Fuck. Tell me you're all right.'

'I'm fine.'

'Where are you?'

'Sidcot.'

'Fucking hell. I thought you were . . .'

'I'm fine, really, Jane. They just wanted a chat.'

'I nearly shit myself.'

'You and me both.'

'I called it in. I'd better let them know you're OK.'

'I'll be in the Sidcot Arms.'

'I'm on my way.'

Dixon was on his second pint by the time Jane arrived at the Sidcot Arms. She ran over and threw her arms around him. Tears were streaming down her face.

'I thought you were . . .'

'I'm fine, really.'

Dixon put his right arm around Jane and kissed her.

'What did they want?'

'Just a chat.'

'A chat?'

'I met the big cheese. He wanted to tell me that our interests did not conflict. That was the phrase he used.'

'What does that mean?'

'That they didn't kill Noel and would I please leave them in peace. That was the gist of it.'

'Did you believe him?'

'I did, as it happens. But then I did before I was kidnapped at gunpoint.'

'What about the betting and the drugs?'

'They know the betting scam is finished. Hesp will take the fall for that. We didn't discuss the drugs. I thought it best not to let on I knew about that.'

'Very wise,' replied Jane. 'What were they like?'

Dixon shook his head.

'I'm not sure, really. Polite and courteous but intimidating with it. Pleasantly threatening. Does that make sense?'

'No. I need a drink.'

'Gin and tonic?'

'Yes, please.'

Dixon was standing at the bar when his phone rang. It was Roger Poland.

'Hello, Roger.'

'Where were you yesterday? I called round about sixish.'

'We stayed at Jane's flat.'

'You all right? I heard about the break in.'

'Fine, thanks.'

'Where are you now?'

'Sidcot.'

'Sidcot? What are you doing there?'

'Long story.'

'Listen, I had the dung sample from Noel's mouth tested by a veterinary pathologist. It's consistent with Dodson & Horrell Race-horse Mix, not the Cubes.'

'So, it's not Westbrook Warrior's?'

'No, it isn't. SOCO found blood on the wheelbarrow so I'm thinking he fell forward onto it and got a mouthful. Either way, it wasn't in Westbrook Warrior's stable, that's for sure.'

'Anything else?'

'The bite was definitely post mortem,' replied Poland. 'And around each horseshoe imprint on the body is the faint outline of a square.'

'A square what?'

'That's your department. It'll be whatever the shoe was nailed to I expect. It's roughly the same width as the shoe.'

'Can you email me a photo?'

'Yes, of course. I'll do it first thing in the morning.'

'Great, thanks.'

Dixon rang off, paid for the drink and carried it back over to Jane.

'Who was that?'

'Roger.'

Dixon filled her in on the dung sample results and also the square outline around the shoe imprints on Noel's body.

'So, it was nailed to a square piece of wood?' asked Jane.

'Looks like it.'

'Still could have been anything.'

'It could.'

'C'mon, drink up and let's get out of here,' said Dixon.

'Where are we going?'

'We'll be safe at the cottage now, unless you'd rather go to your flat.'

'The flat.'

They were walking across the car park to Dixon's Land Rover when his phone rang again. This time it was DCI Lewis.

'Are you all right?'

'Yes, Sir.'

'What the bloody hell's been going on?'

'I was picked up by the Albanians, but they just wanted a chat, Sir. I'll fill you in tomorrow.'

'Where are you now?'

'Sidcot.'

'Is Jane there?'

'She is.'

'What's happening now?'

'We're going home, Sir.'

'Good. And for heaven's sake, stay out of trouble.'

Chapter Eight

'Georgina Harcourt rang last night, Sir.'

'What?'

'At 9.37 p.m. Mrs Georgina Harcourt. No message, no number.'

Louise Willmott handed the note to Dixon.

'Why wasn't this passed on?'

'Don't know, Sir.'

'Well, find out, will you? And remind them this is a bloody murder investigation.'

Dixon and Jane had arrived at Bridgwater Police Station just after 8.30 a.m. Louise Willmott was waiting for them but otherwise the CID Room was empty. They made themselves a coffee and checked their emails while they waited for Louise. She reappeared a few minutes later.

'They didn't think . . .'

'Didn't think? If anyone else says that to me I'm gonna . . .'

Dixon screwed his empty plastic coffee cup into a ball and threw it at the bin in the corner of his office. He missed.

'Get me her phone number, somebody.'

Dixon rang the landline at Gidley's Racing Stables and then Georgina Harcourt's mobile phone number. No reply.

'In here a minute, will you?'

Jane sat at Janice Courtenay's desk and Louise on the chair in front of Dixon's desk.

'Change of direction. You've heard what happened yesterday, Louise?'

'You had a visit from the Albanians.'

'I did,' said Dixon. 'But what it tells me is this: if Noel was about to blab about either the horse racing or the drugs, then he'd be at the bottom of the Bristol Channel by now. Nobody would be any the wiser. He'd just be another missing person.'

'So, the Albanians have got nothing to do with it?' asked Louise.

'I don't think so. This was an amateur job. They're professionals. No traces.'

'Makes sense,' said Jane.

'It does,' said Louise.

'This was someone who knew a little about horses but not enough. Someone who tried to make it look like Westbrook Warrior kicked him to death, and failed dismally.'

'So, what do we do now?' asked Louise.

'I want full background checks on all of the owners and syndicate members. Everyone associated with every horse at that yard. I also want all of their mobile phone records so we can cross check them with Noel's. And Philip Stockman. Let's find him and set up a meeting today.'

'Yes, Sir,' said Jane.

'And Noel's iPad and phone. Have we heard back from High Tech yet, Louise?'

'No, Sir. I'll chase it up.'

'I want all calls to and from Noel's phone checked and cross referenced.'

'So, what do you think the motive is, then?'

'He was a rent boy, Louise. Do you want me to spell it out for you?'

'Blackmail, you mean?'

'It would explain the money, the iPad and PlayStation, wouldn't it? He sure as hell wasn't making that sort of money out of Hesp or Clapham Racing, was he?'

'Was he still selling himself?'

The phone on Dixon's desk rang.

'Possibly, but who to?' replied Dixon.

'Yes, Sir. I'll be along in a minute.'

Dixon hung up.

'A summons. I'll be back in a minute. It's going to be a lot of work and there's only the three of us, so let's get on with it.'

'Tell me about yesterday, then,' said DCI Lewis.

'Not a lot to tell, really, Sir,' replied Dixon. 'Gun in the ribs, in the car, quick chat, out at Sidcot.'

'Don't be ridiculous. Who did you meet and what did he say?'

'He said his name was Zavan.'

'You met the man himself.'

'He knew the betting scam was over. We didn't discuss the drugs. I think he just wanted to make sure I knew they had nothing to do with Noel's death.'

'You believed him?'

'Yes. I'd already ruled it out, actually, having spoken to DCS Collyer.'

'Why?'

'If it was the Albanians, then Noel would have just disappeared, wouldn't he?'

Lewis nodded.

'Clean and simple. No traces,' said Dixon.

'And what did you tell him?'

'Nothing he didn't already know.'

'So, it was all a bit of a waste of time?'

'It cured my constipation but that's about it, Sir.'

Lewis roared with laughter.

'Collyer's been on. Wanted to know why you haven't told him about it yet.'

'Tell him I didn't think, Sir,' said Dixon, closing the door behind him.

'Right, you know what you've got to do, then, Louise?'

'Yes, Sir.'

'C'mon then, Jane, let's get going.'

Jane looked up from her computer.

'Where are we . . . ?'

'See Georgina Harcourt. She must have rung for a reason.'

They sped west out of Bridgwater on the now familiar Durleigh Road. It was raining hard and Jane had the Land Rover's windscreen wipers working at full speed. Dark grey clouds were racing low across the sky and not a single sailing dinghy was braving the waves out on the reservoir.

They arrived at Gidley's Racing Stables to find the car park empty, apart from Michael Hesp's Toyota Land Cruiser. Both horse lorries were parked on the hard standing off to the left of the entrance, all locked up this time. Dixon and Jane walked into the courtyard and stood under the stable block canopy just inside the entrance. They could see the horses in their stables, including Westbrook Warrior behind his metal grille.

Dixon looked up at the farmhouse to his left. No lights were on inside, which surprised him, given that it was such a dark morning. He nudged Jane and then both of them walked across the courtyard and up the stone steps to the front door. Dixon stood under the porch, listening.

'Is that her car over there?' he said, pointing to a dark green Nissan Micra parked at the side of the house.

'Yes.'

Dixon rang the doorbell and waited. Nothing. It was a loud bell that would have been heard by anyone in the house.

'Not in.'

'Or not in to visitors,' said Jane.

Dixon rang the doorbell again and knocked on the door loudly. The door knocker was solid brass so he gave it a good clatter. Still no response. Dixon tried the door. It was locked.

'Wait here,' he said.

Dixon walked down the steps and across the courtyard. He then turned into the alleyway at the far end of Westbrook Warrior's stable block. He paused at the end, sheltering from the rain and listening. The muckheap off to his right was deserted but he could hear voices in the American barn to his left.

Hesp was in a stable with Kevin Tanner and both appeared to be examining the back leg of a large grey horse.

'This'll be Uphill Tobermory, I suppose,' said Dixon.

The look of surprise on Hesp's face did not go unnoticed.

'Er, yes,' replied Hesp. 'Picked up a bit of a strain on the gallops yesterday, I think. Nothing serious.'

Hesp turned back to the horse and began running his right hand up and down its hind leg.

'I'm looking for Mrs Harcourt,' said Dixon.

'In the house, I expect. I've not seen her today.'

'She's not answering the door.'

'She may have taken one of her sleeping pills, then.'

'I need to speak to her.'

'The back door should be open,' said Hesp, without looking up.

'Thank you.'

Dixon ran back through the alleyway, along the front of the stable block and then up the stone steps.

'Round the back,' he said to Jane.

He walked along the front of the house and followed the path around to the back. Jane was behind him. They came to a timber framed porch that looked as if it was about to collapse. The door was ajar. Inside were several pairs of Wellington and riding boots on the dirty tiled floor and assorted leather tack on a shelf. Too many coats were hanging on too few hooks.

The inner door was closed. Dixon tried the handle. It turned and the door opened.

'I don't like the sniff of this,' he said.

'Me neither,' said Jane.

Dixon stepped into the kitchen. It was much the same as before. Filthy.

'Mrs Harcourt?' he shouted.

No response.

He walked across the kitchen and stood in the doorway leading to the hall.

'Mrs Harcourt?'

Still nothing.

He checked the ground floor rooms, first the living room, then the dining room and office. Nothing. Dixon looked up the stairs.

'Let's hope she's asleep.'

They crept up the stairs and stood on the large galleried landing. There were three doors to their left, at the front of the house, and two to their right.

'Hesp said her bedroom was at the back,' said Jane.

Dixon took his left arm out of the sling and then walked towards one of the back bedroom doors. He opened it and looked in.

'Empty.'

Jane opened the next door.

'This is it. She's still in bed.'

Dixon peered over Jane's shoulder.

'She looks asleep. Wake her up.'

Jane stepped forward and stood over Mrs Harcourt. The bed covers were pulled up over her shoulders and only her head was visible on the pillow. Her eyes were closed and she was lying on her back with her head tipped to the left.

'She's not breathing.'

Dixon switched the light on.

'No, she's dead,' said Jane. 'She's white as a sheet.'

Dixon stood at the end of the bed. He could see immediately that Georgina Harcourt was dead and had been for some time. On her bedside table was a box of pills, presumably her sleeping pills, and a half bottle of whisky. It was empty.

'Call it in,' said Dixon. 'Get her doctor here. We'll need SOCO and Roger as well.'

Jane went out onto the landing and dialled 999. Dixon could hear her talking in the background but he wasn't listening to her conversation. He stood at the end of Georgina Harcourt's bed. She looked at peace. She may not have enjoyed restful sleep in life, but she was getting plenty of it now, he thought.

Jane came back into the room.

'An ambulance and backup are on the way. James Davidson too.'

'Thanks, but no thanks. It needs to be Roger. Ring him direct.'

Jane shrugged her shoulders and went out onto the landing to ring Roger Poland.

Dixon looked around the room. Something was missing. He checked the bedside table and the dresser.

'Roger's on his way,' said Jane. 'He's ringing Davidson and putting him off.'

'Good. See if you can find a suicide note, will you? Try downstairs. Kitchen table, office, perhaps, maybe the coffee table in the living room.'

'OK.'

Dixon looked at the sleeping tablets: Restoril. He leaned over and looked into the open box. It was empty. Next to it on the bedside table were four empty sleeves of pills. Twenty in each, making a total of eighty sleeping pills, possibly, and a half bottle of whisky.

Dixon shouted down the stairs.

'Jane?'

'Yes.'

'Is her doctor on the way?'

'They were going to try and get hold of him.'

'Ring them again and tell them to get him here. Now.'

'Will do.'

Dixon went downstairs and looked around the living room. He looked at the drinks cabinet, against the wall behind the sofa. The bottles were lined up on top of it, next to three empty decanters that were covered in dust. The cupboards underneath contained only glasses and an unopened bottle of Stone's ginger wine. Dixon made a note of the bottles on the top of the cabinet. Gin, vodka, port, several bottles of slimline tonic with lime zest, a bottle of Bacardi and an empty bottle of Diet Coke. No whisky.

He looked in the kitchen. In amongst the dirty pans and plates he could see several empty bottles of red wine and two unopened ones. There were two bottles of Pinot Grigio in the fridge, one half empty.

'Let's go and have a word with Mr Hesp.'

It was still raining hard, so they walked along the front of the stables, sheltering under the canopy. Dixon spotted Kevin Tanner in the feed store and he pointed them in the direction of the American barn, where they found Hesp bandaging the hind leg of Uphill Tobermory.

'May we have a word, please, Mr Hesp?'

'I'll be with you in a minute.'

'Now.'

Hesp looked up. Dixon was standing by the stable door.

'What can possibly be that urgent?'

'Mrs Harcourt is dead, Mr Hesp.'

'Georgina? How?'

'We don't know yet. Now, if we could have a word, please, up at the house?'

'Yes. Yes, of course.'

They walked back along the alleyway and up to the farm-house. As they walked past the feed store, Hesp shouted across to Kevin Tanner.

'Kevin, finish bandaging up Toby's leg, will you?'

'OK.'

Once in the kitchen, Hesp sat down at the table.

'We'll use the living room, I think,' said Dixon.

Hesp sat on the sofa. Dixon stood opposite him with his back to the fireplace. Jane sat on an armchair, notebook at the ready.

'Where were you last night, Mr Hesp?' asked Dixon.

'Wait a minute, you can't possibly think that I . . . ?'

'Where were you?'

'I stayed at a friend's house in Taunton.'

'Name?'

'She's married.'

Dixon looked through the front window and saw a police car and an ambulance pull into the courtyard.

'How did she die?' asked Hesp.

'It's too early to say, I'm afraid, Mr Hesp,' replied Dixon. 'What time did you leave last night?'

'About 7.30. Once we'd finished for the night.'

'And when did you get back?'

'This morning. Sevenish. In time to help Kevin with the feeding.'

'When did you last see Mrs Harcourt?'

'Yesterday, late afternoon, say, fiveish. I came in for a cup of tea. Then she went out in her car and got back after I left, I suppose. I didn't see her after that.'

'How was she when you saw her?'

'What do you mean?'

'Her mood. How did she seem?'

'Fine. Her usual self. Why?'

There was a knock at the front door.

'Excuse me, Mr Hesp. We'll continue this in a moment.'

Dixon and Jane left Michael Hesp in the living room.

'Jane, get a statement from Tanner. See if he can shed any light on Mrs Harcourt's movements yesterday afternoon and whether he confirms Hesp's story.'

'OK.'

Dixon spoke to the two paramedics and the uniformed officer who had arrived.

'At the moment, I want this treated as an unexplained death. Disturb as little as you can and watch out for anything that might be evidence.'

'Yes, Sir.'

Dixon followed the paramedics upstairs. They pulled the duvet cover back far enough to check Mrs Harcourt's vital signs before confirming that she was dead. Dixon then left the uniformed officer guarding the room.

He watched the ambulance back out of the courtyard from the living room window.

'I'm going to need your friend's name, Mr Hesp.'

'I can't . . .'

'We'll be discreet.'

'Why?'

'Let's just say that Mrs Harcourt's death is currently unexplained and it may help to eliminate you from our enquiries.'

'Miriam Sims. She lives at 37 Bennet Avenue.'

'How often do you stay with Mrs Sims?'

'Whenever her husband's away. He's a diver on the oil rigs. He works a month on, month off.'

'Thank you.'

———⌣———

'What've we got, then?' asked Poland. 'This is supposed to be my day off.'

'Mrs Georgina Harcourt. Dead in bed upstairs. She owns the place and rents it to the trainer, Michael Hesp. We interviewed her a couple of days ago and she denied any knowledge of the betting scam and any involvement in Noel's death. I've since learned that she at least knew about the drugs.'

'Drugs?'

'In the horse lorries.'

Poland shook his head.

'Was she involved?'

'I don't think so. She knew about it but that's all. She rang the station last night, asking for me, but the message wasn't passed on. Next thing we know, she's dead. You'll see what it looks like . . .'

'I get the picture. Lead on.'

They stood in the doorway of the bedroom watching the scientific services team at work. One was taking photographs and the other dusting the bedside table for fingerprints.

'You finished?'

'Almost, Sir.'

Dixon stood behind Poland as he surveyed the scene. The whisky bottle and sleeping pills were in separate evidence bags.

'Restoril. Temazepam is the active ingredient. It's a benzo-diazepine usually used as a sleeping pill. Fatal in sufficient quantity, especially when mixed with half a bottle of Scotch.'

Poland pulled back the duvet. Georgina Harcourt was lying on her back. Her right arm was at her side and her left across her chest. Her eyes and mouth were closed.

'She looks asleep, doesn't she?' said Dixon.

'That's what happens. You go to sleep,' replied Poland, 'then the breathing goes.'

'Any sign of foul play?'

'What makes you think . . . ?'

'She tried to ring me at 9.37 last night. Then this.'

'But . . .'

'And there's no suicide note.'

'That doesn't prove anything. You know the statistics for that.'

'These Albanians are good, Roger. They'd know she took sleep-ing pills. She takes a pill and is sound asleep. They creep in. Two hold her down. Two others pour the pills and Scotch down her throat, using a funnel so there's no mess. She wouldn't have stood a chance.'

'But, there's no sign of restraint . . .'

'What if they were wearing soft gloves when they held her wrists? That wouldn't leave a mark.'

'No, it wouldn't, I suppose.'

'And the Scotch. She was a drinker. You only have to look in the living room to see that. But there's no sign of whisky anywhere.'

The uniformed officer appeared in the doorway.

'Her doctor's here, Sir.'

'Send him up, will you?'

'Yes, Sir.'

'So, what you're saying is that we've got no suicide note and she didn't like whisky, therefore it must be murder. Is that it?' asked Poland.

'I wouldn't have put it quite like that . . .'

'You're clutching at straws, Nick.'

'I'm Doctor Carpenter, Mrs Harcourt's GP.'

'Come in,' said Dixon.

'It's very sad. I always hate suicides,' said Carpenter. '"Never commit suicide; you might regret it later".'

'Who said that?'

'Winston Churchill, I think. He was talking political suicide, but it still applies.'

'It does,' replied Dixon. 'Forgive me, I'm Detective Inspector Dixon and this is Roger Poland, pathologist at Musgrove Park.'

They shook hands.

'Scotch and Restoril,' said Poland. 'Had you prescribed her Restoril?'

'Yes. I started her on Zopiclone but after a while it didn't work for her so we tried Restoril.'

'There are eighty here. Could she have stockpiled that many?'

'Yes, probably. She's been on it for a while.'

'Did she have any problems with alcohol?'

'Not that she told me about. She was a social drinker. Nothing excessive, that I saw.'

'Any other medication,' asked Poland.

'She took a statin but apart from that, no.'

'What about her mental state?'

'Prone to bouts of depression, but nothing too dramatic. I seem to recall one prescription of Fluoxetine some time ago, but that's it.'

'What's that?' asked Dixon.

'The trade name is Prozac,' replied Poland.

Dixon nodded.

'Thank you, Doctor,' said Poland.

Dr Carpenter left and Poland turned to Dixon.

'I've got to do a PM anyway so I'll keep an eye out for anything suspicious but I think you are way off the mark with this one, Nick.'

'Looks like it. I've just got this alarm bell going off . . .'

'Even if you're right, there's no physical evidence to prove it.'

'So, if it was murder…?' asked Dixon.

'. . . It was a thoroughly professional job,' replied Poland.

———

Dixon stood under the canopy on the corner of the stable block and watched Georgina Harcourt being carried out of the farmhouse to the waiting mortuary van. It looked disturbingly similar to the Albanians' Range Rover. Black with tinted windows. The Scientific Services van had left a few minutes before and Roger Poland was almost finished at the scene as well. The next step would be the post mortem. He shouted across to Dixon.

'I'll let you know if I find anything.'

'Thank you.'

'You owe me another one for this.'

'Curry?'

'After last time?'

Poland followed the mortuary van out of the courtyard on foot and got in his car. Then he sped off down the drive after the van. Dixon looked at his watch. It was nearly midday.

'Let's get some lunch.'

'OK,' replied Jane.

———

'What d'you make of it, then?' asked Dixon.

'If it wasn't for the telephone call the night before, I'd say it was suicide. That's the only issue for me. It still could have been suicide, couldn't it? But . . . maybe she couldn't live with whatever it was she was going to tell us?'

'Or maybe she was killed for it?'

'It's a tricky one,' said Jane.

They were sitting at a small table in the corner of an otherwise deserted lounge bar in the Lamb in Spaxton. A dreary Monday lunchtime in November was clearly not their busiest time. Two cheese sandwiches and a bowl of chips arrived.

'She couldn't just disappear after Zavan told me that was their speciality. So it had to look like suicide . . .' Dixon's voice tailed off.

'What?'

'Do you remember when Collyer said that Georgina was a reluctant participant in whatever was going on, or something like that? I asked him how he knew . . .'

'And he said "we listen". I wondered what he meant by that.'

'I reckon they've got the house bugged.'

'Zephyr?'

'Yes.'

'Could just be a telephone tap,' said Jane.

'We'll get Lewis to find out. About time he did something useful.'

Jane parked on the pavement outside the Glastonbury Music Shop in Benedict Street, a narrow side road off Market Place, Glastonbury. A little further down, on the opposite side of the street, was a red brick terraced cottage with hanging baskets either side of the front door. It had once been a residential address but was now the offices of Stockman Accountancy Services, as evidenced by the brass plaque on the wall. Dixon moved the flowers to one side and read aloud from the plaque.

'Philip Stockman FCA, trading as Stockman Accountancy Services.'

'FCA?' asked Jane.

'Fellow of the Institute of Chartered Accountants.'

Dixon tried to peer through the front window, but it was obscured by a dirty net curtain. He tried the door, which was locked, so Jane rang the doorbell.

The door was answered by a woman in her early sixties, smartly dressed in a two piece navy wool suit.

'We're looking for Philip Stockman,' said Dixon.

'Is he expecting you?'

'Yes. I am Detective Inspector Dixon and this is Detective Constable Winter. We have an appointment at 2 p.m.'

'He sends his apologies, I'm afraid. He wasn't feeling well and has gone home.'

'Where does he live?'

'I'm afraid I can't . . .'

Dixon closed his eyes and took a deep breath. It was enough to stop the woman mid-sentence.

'Let me explain. This is a murder investigation, Mrs . . . ?'

'Stevens. Ms Stevens.'

Dixon showed her his warrant card.

'Now, I can get his address the hard way, unless you'd like to save me the trouble.'

'Beck House. It's off Turnhill Road, High Ham.'

'Do you know it, Jane?'

'I know High Ham.'

'Head out of the village on Turnhill Road. It's about five hundred yards on the left. A gravel drive. If you reach the sharp right hand bend, you've gone too far.'

'And what did he say was wrong with him?'

Hesitation. 'A headache.'

'Thank you, Ms Stevens.'

———⌣———

'I bet she rings him,' said Jane, as they drove out of Glastonbury.

'Of course she will. She's got to tell him what's wrong with him, for a start. But if he's done a bunk before we get there, he's got something to hide, hasn't he?'

'He has.'

'C'mon, Jane, step on it. This isn't an old milk float, you know.'

'Might just as well be.'

It took no more than ten minutes to find Beck House. They turned into the drive and, for once, noise from outside the car drowned out the diesel engine. Dixon was surprised at how loud crunching gravel could be. It would certainly announce their arrival to anyone in the house.

Jane parked next to a red BMW estate. Dixon looked up at the large grey stone double fronted manor with a columned porch.

'Plenty of money in accountancy, isn't there?'

'He may have inherited it,' replied Jane.

The front door of the house opened and a man wearing a red silk dressing gown stepped out and waited under the porch. He was in his late fifties or early sixties, with very short grey hair. A number two cut with clippers, thought Dixon.

'Nice of him to get off his death bed just for us, isn't it?'

'Behave,' said Jane.

Dixon glanced into the back of the Land Rover as he got out. Monty was fast asleep.

'Mr Stockman?'

'I'm sorry to have mucked you about. I've got one of my migraines.'

'That's all right, Sir, we won't keep you long,' replied Dixon, handing his warrant card to Philip Stockman. 'May we come in?'

Stockman did not reply. He stood staring down at Dixon's warrant card. When he looked up, there were tears in his eyes.

'I loved him, you know.'

'Noel?'

'Yes. He didn't love me, though. I was just a meal ticket.'

'Shall we go inside, Mr Stockman?'

'Yes, sorry. Come in.'

Dixon and Jane followed Stockman into the living room. There was a large sofa opposite an open fire with an ornate marble mantelpiece. Above that was hanging a huge gilt framed mirror. At the front of the room was a large bay window with full height sash windows and velvet curtains.

'This is a beautiful room,' said Jane.

'Thank you,' replied Stockman.

Jane sat on the sofa next to Philip Stockman. Dixon stood looking out of the window before sitting on the window seat.

'You were saying about Noel . . .'

'There's not a lot else to say, really.'

'When did you meet him?'

'Two years ago, give or take.'

'Where?'

'We met in the car park. That's where I meet all my friends.'

'Which car park?'

'On the A39. Just by the bridge there over the King's Sedgemoor Drain.'

'Were you a customer of his?'

'Only the first time.'

'Then he moved in here?'

'Not straight away, but eventually I persuaded him to.'

'Where was he living at the time?'

'I don't know. He moved around.'

'And when he came here, what happened?'

'I gave him money. Trying to stop him . . . selling himself. I could cope with the infidelity. Just not the risk.'

'And did he stop?'

'For a while. Until one day he came home all battered and bruised and I knew he'd been doing it again.'

'Why?'

'What do you mean?'

'Well, you were giving him money . . .'

'It was the danger, Inspector. He loved the danger of it.'

'How did he come to get involved with horses?'

'I used to go riding and he came with me a few times. He was a good rider. Confident in the saddle. So I introduced him to Georgina Harcourt. I thought it would give him a sense of direction, and it did. The first time he rode a horse on the gallops there, he was hooked.'

'The speed?'

'Yes. He must have been an adrenaline junkie, or whatever they call it.'

'What happened then?'

'He got the job there and went to live in that stinking caravan. But he loved being near the horses.'

'Did you keep in touch?'

'Yes. We'd meet up occasionally. I saw him in the car park once so I knew he was up to his old tricks too. He didn't see me, thankfully.'

'When was the last time you saw him?'

'Two weeks before he died. He came here for the weekend.'

'Did he ever mention anyone in particular? Someone who had been violent towards him, perhaps?'

'No. We never spoke about his other encounters.'

'What about money?'

'He didn't ask for any and I didn't offer it. He was getting paid by Michael Hesp, don't forget.'

'Would it surprise you to learn that he had an iPad, a PlayStation and six hundred quid's worth of Canon digital camera?'

'Yes, it would. Definitely,' replied Stockman. 'Where on earth did he get that lot from, I wonder?'

'That's what we need to find out,' replied Dixon. 'And you know Georgina Harcourt?'

'Yes, we've been friends for years.'

'Well, I'm sorry to have to tell you, Mr Stockman, but Mrs Harcourt is dead.'

'What?'

'She was found this morning, in her bed. I'm afraid that it looks like suicide.'

Jane looked at Dixon and raised her eyebrows. Philip Stockman began to sob.

'Does that surprise you?'

'What?'

'That Mrs Harcourt committed suicide?'

'It saddens me. No, it doesn't surprise me. She'd been unhappy for some time, bless her.'

'Did she tell you why?'

'No. Which is odd because we used to talk about anything and everything, but I could never get her to open up about it.'

'It?'

'Whatever it was that was bothering her.'

'Did she like whisky?'

'What an odd question?'

'Humour me.'

'No. She hated it. Never touched the stuff.'

'Thank you, Mr Stockman. I think we've taken up enough of your time. You'll be wanting to get back to bed, I expect.'

Jane waited until the Land Rover was off the gravel drive.

'What was all that about suicide?'

'I never thought much about your murder theory, to be honest, Jane. It's interesting that she hated whisky but it's the only thing you've got on your side. You have to admit, it's pretty thin, isn't it?'

'Git.'

'Let's get back to the station and see what Louise has been able to rustle up.'

Chapter Nine

'There's nothing on the camera or the iPad, but we've got two numbers unaccounted for on Noel's phone,' said Louise.

'Two?'

'Yes, all the rest we can identify. His brother and sister, Kevin Tanner, Clapham, Hesp and Philip Stockman. There are a couple of landlines too. His doctor, father's house and Stockman's office.'

'Father's house?' asked Jane.

'Don't forget Natalie lives there,' said Dixon.

Jane nodded.

'What about these other two, then?' continued Dixon.

'One's a Vodafone number. I've been onto them and am just waiting for a call back. The other is an unregistered pay as you go number with Tesco Mobile.'

'Buy it at the checkout. Stick some money on it and then away you go. Untraceable,' said Dixon.

'Here's the list,' said Louise, passing the printout to Dixon. 'Dates, times and call length.'

'Get onto the phone networks. We need positioning records for both numbers when the calls were made and received. I want to know where Noel was when he rang that number and where that number was when it received his call. OK?'

'Can they do that?'

'Yes. A mobile phone communicates with any base station within range. The strongest signal will be with the nearest base station and then you triangulate from there. It'll give us a rough idea where he was.'

'But in the countryside the base stations are further apart . . . ?'

'They are, Jane. I did say a rough idea.'

'DCI Lewis will need to authorise it, surely?' asked Jane.

'It'll come from higher up the food chain, but he can sort it out,' replied Dixon. 'What about the background checks on everyone else, Louise?'

'Still working on it, Sir.'

Dixon looked at his watch. It was nearly 4.30 p.m.

'How far have you got?'

'I've got a list of names and addresses, landlines where they've got them, and mobile phone numbers. I've also got their previous convictions where they're known to us, and I've been digging around on the Internet, too. Employment, businesses, company directorships, that sort of thing.'

'How many are there?'

'Lots. Sixteen horses, eleven private owners and five syndicates. A total of forty-two people.'

'Shit,' said Jane.

'We've got our work cut out then, haven't we?' said Dixon.

The phone rang on Janice Courtenay's desk. Louise answered it. 'Yes.'

She reached for a notepad and pen and began making notes.

'Thank you very much.'

She rang off.

'Jason Freer. Vodafone contract customer. Lives at 51 Berryvale Avenue, Bridgwater.'

'Well done, Louise,' said Dixon.

Dixon looked at Jane.

'Don't just sit there then, go and interview him,' he said. 'And take Louise with you.'

'Me?' asked Louise.

'Yes, you. It's about time you got out and about a bit.'

Jane looked at Louise and shrugged her shoulders. They got up and left.

Dixon made himself a coffee from the machine and then turned back to the list of mobile phone calls. It started with the most recent and worked backwards. He highlighted the calls Noel made to and received from the unidentified pay as you go number and wrote them out on a separate piece of paper. He reversed the order of the list so that they now appeared in chronological order, starting with the first. Dates, times and call length. Made or received.

He sat staring at it for several minutes.

'You all right?'

Dixon looked up. DCI Lewis was standing in the doorway of his office.

'Yes, Sir. Thank you.'

Lewis turned to walk away.

'Could I have a word with you, Sir?'

'Of course,' said Lewis, walking into Dixon's office and closing the door behind him. He sat down on the chair in front of Dixon's desk.

'What's up?'

'You're going to get a request for mobile phone positioning records. I know it's expensive, but it's all we've got at the moment.'

'Those have to be approved by the chief super.'

'Yes, but she'll ask your advice . . .'

'She will.'

155

Dixon raised his eyebrows.

'Leave it with me,' said Lewis. 'Anything else?'

'Yes. Georgina Harcourt . . .'

'The suicide?'

'It's looking increasingly like it. But she hated whisky, so why did she use that? And why did she call me on Sunday night? Bit of a coincidence, isn't it.'

'Poland found anything?'

'Not yet.'

'Maybe she wanted to make a deathbed confession?'

'Maybe she did. Anyway, when Collyer came to see me in the hospital, he said that she was a reluctant player in the drugs. She knew about it but wasn't actively involved. I asked him how he knew and he said "we listen". So, I'm thinking . . .'

'They've got the house bugged?'

'It's possible,' said Dixon.

'It's illegal,' replied Lewis.

'Needs must.'

'Anything you got from it would be inadmissible.'

'I'm only after a point in the right direction, Sir.'

'The more likely explanation is a telephone tap, which would give you nothing.'

'It's worth asking, surely?'

'All right, I'll see what I can find out.'

'Thank you, Sir.'

'Is that it?'

'Yes.'

'I'll leave you to it, then,' said Lewis, getting up.

Dixon turned back to his handwritten list of telephone calls and began staring at it again.

Berryvale Avenue was a narrow tree lined road of former council houses towards the north of Bridgwater. Cars were parked on the pavement either side of the road. Number 51 was at the far end, close to the junction with Osborne Road. It had a chicken wire fence around what lawn was visible under rusting car parts, two motorcycles, a small caravan that had collapsed on its wheels, and a fridge.

The tiny patches of lawn that were clear of rubbish were enough to tell Jane that a large dog also lived in the house.

It was just getting dark when she knocked on the door. She stopped when loud barking started.

'There's a surprise,' said Jane. 'You all right with dogs?'

'Fine,' replied Louise.

They listened at the door and heard a man shouting.

'Come here. Come . . . Right, now, get in there.' Then the sound of a door being closed.

'That's a relief,' said Jane.

Louise smiled.

A figure appeared behind the frosted glass of the front door. Jane could pick out blue trousers, probably jeans, a red shirt and dark hair. The door opened. Jane immediately recognised the telltale smell of marijuana and could see a cloud of smoke coming from the kitchen at the back of the house.

'Jason Freer?' asked Jane.

'Who wants to know?'

She held up her warrant card.

'It's personal use . . .'

'I'm not interested in that. Are you Jason Freer?'

'Yes.'

'We'd like a word about Noel Woodman. May we come in?'

'Give me a minute,' said Freer, closing the door.

Jane could hear muffled voices and then the back door being opened and closed again.

'The dope fiends make their escape.'

'They'll be back,' said Louise.

'And so will we,' replied Jane, 'when they least expect it.'

Louise grinned.

Freer opened the front door. 'You'd better come in.'

'Thank you, Mr Freer,' replied Jane.

They stepped into the hall.

'I am Detective Constable Winter and this is Police Constable Willmott.'

'We'll use the kitchen. Luka's in there,' said Freer, pointing at the living room door.

'And what is Luka?'

'A Rottweiler.'

They walked along the hall to the kitchen. Louise and Freer sat either side of the small kitchen table. Jane stood by the sink. Louise was taking notes.

'When did you last see Noel?'

'Three or four weeks ago. What's he been up to now?'

'He's dead, Mr Freer.'

'Dead?'

'Murdered, to be precise.'

'Oh, shit,' said Freer. He reached for a packet of cigarettes on the table. Jane could see that he was trembling as he fumbled with the lighter.

'How did you know him?' asked Jane.

'What . . . what happened to him?'

'How did you know him, please, Mr Freer?'

'We met in a car park on the A39. Same line of work, you might say.'

'Sex workers?' asked Jane.

'Yes.'

'When was that?'

'About three years ago. He'd left home.'

'How . . . ?'

'Actually, he'd been thrown out. He hadn't left.'

'How well did you know him?'

'We used to look out for each other, you know. It can be dangerous. He got beaten up a few times. It's happened to me too. So we'd keep an eye out for each other.'

'Who beat him up, do you know?'

'No. Just random punters.'

'Where was he living?'

'He moved around. It was a way of getting a bed for the night. Sometimes he stayed here.'

'How often?'

'A couple of times.'

'Did you have a sexual relationship with him?'

Freer shook his head.

'Did he have any regular clients?'

'Not to begin with. Then he met Philip.'

'Philip Stockman?'

'I never knew his surname.'

'What happened then?'

'He went to live over Glastonbury way. I didn't see him for a while after that. Then he began showing up again.'

'When was this?'

'Eighteen months or so ago. He said he was working at a stables and the pay was shit.'

'How often would you see him then?'

'Not as often as before. Maybe once or twice a week at first.'

'What do you mean, "at first"?'

'The last maybe year or so, he's not been so often.'

'How often?'

'Once a month.'

'So, let me make sure I've got this right,' said Jane. 'He's a regular at the car park until he meets Philip Stockman. Then he's not there at all for a while?'

'Yes.'

'Then, when he starts coming back, he's there once or twice a week, but for the last year or so it's only been once a month.'

'If that, thinking about it,' replied Freer.

'What changed, then?' asked Jane.

'I don't know.'

'Tell me about his clients.'

'Different cars, different people.'

'No regulars?'

'Philip.'

'When he started coming back, I mean?'

'Yeah, there was then.'

'Who?'

'Don't know.'

'He never spoke to you about this person?'

'No.'

'Can you remember the car?'

'I seem to remember a four wheel drive but I may have got that wrong.'

'So, what you're saying is when he started coming back, when he was at the stables, he had a regular client, then about a year ago he stopped almost completely?'

'He still came from time to time, but he didn't need the money anymore, he said. It was just for the fun of it.'

'Why not?'

'He had a new meal ticket.'

'Meal ticket?'

'Those were his words exactly.'

'You've got no idea who this person might be?'

'No.'

'Let's be quite clear that it's not Philip Stockman we're talking about, is it?'

'No. That was before.'

'And he was getting money from this person?'

'Yes.'

'Did he say how much?'

'No, but I got the impression it was quite a lot.'

'Was he a client?'

'I assume so.'

'Did Noel say anything else that might be relevant?'

'Not that I can think of.'

'OK, we'll leave you to it, Mr Freer, but if you think of anything else . . .'

'And you're not interested in the . . . er . . . ?'

'No, we're not interested in that.'

'Thanks,' replied Freer.

⌣

Dixon was still staring at his handwritten list of mobile phone calls when Jane and Louise arrived back at Bridgwater Police Station. There were three empty plastic coffee cups on the desk in front of him.

'You've been busy, I see,' said Jane.

'Took Monty for a walk, though. Remembered that,' replied Dixon.

Louise walked into Dixon's office and sat at Janice Courtenay's desk.

'Well, what'd you get?' asked Dixon.

'He enjoys his weed, does Mr Freer,' said Louise.

'Jason Freer is a rent boy. He and Noel used to work the car park on the A39. They looked out for each other, apparently,' said Jane.

'Give me the bones of it,' said Dixon.

'Well, Freer remembers Noel meeting Philip Stockman. After that he didn't see him for a while. Then he started appearing in the car park again. Noel told him he was working at some stables and the pay was shit.'

Dixon nodded.

'This was about eighteen months ago,' continued Jane. 'He had a regular client, too. Freer couldn't recall anything about him, but he did remember that Noel stopped showing up at the car park almost completely about a year ago. He'd see him once a month or so after that.'

'Do we know why that was?' asked Dixon.

'Noel told Freer he had a new meal ticket and didn't need the money anymore.'

'A new meal ticket . . .' Dixon's voice tailed off. 'A year ago, you say?'

'Yes,' replied Jane.

Dixon looked at the list of mobile phone calls.

'That was when these calls started,' he said. 'The ones to and from the unregistered pay as you go.'

'Same man?' asked Louise.

'Let's assume so, for the time being. How much money was he getting?'

'Freer didn't know but said he thought it was . . .'

'Quite a lot, was the phrase he used,' said Louise, looking at her notes.

'Enough for an iPad and PlayStation,' said Dixon.

'And that camera,' said Jane.

'So, Noel's blackmailing someone and is killed for it. It's a regular punter of his . . .' Dixon piled up his empty coffee cups, one inside the other. Then he walked over to the other side of his office and dropped them in the bin. 'The key is in these phone calls.'

'Must be,' replied Jane.

'Good work, the pair of you,' said Dixon.

'Thank you, Sir,' said Louise.

'I've spoken to DCI Lewis about the mobile positioning, Louise. He'll clear it with the chief super for us if you can get the details over to him straight away.'

'Yes, Sir.'

Dixon looked at his watch. It was nearly 7.30 p.m.

'Then you'd better go home. Be back here at 8 a.m. sharp.'

'Will do.'

Jane waited until Louise had left Dixon's office.

'What are we gonna do?'

'Your place or mine?'

———

Dixon took his left arm out of the sling and tried stretching his shoulder as much as he could. He was sitting in the living room at Jane's flat in Bridgwater.

'Feels a bit better,' he said.

'Good,' said Jane, pouring two large glasses of red wine.

She looked over at Monty, curled up on the rug in front of the fire. It was an artificial fireplace and an electric fire, but Monty didn't know or care.

'A tiny little house and a garden full of rubbish and that idiot Freer's got a Rottweiler living there.'

'Did you see it?'

'No, but we'll be going back as soon as this is over. Louise and I came out of there as high as kites just from the fumes.'

Dixon laughed. Jane sat on the sofa next to him and then turned to face him. She put her legs across his lap.

'What's going on in there?' asked Jane, tapping Dixon on the side of his head with her finger.

'We've had an armed siege, a betting scam, drug smuggling and organised crime all thrown in and it's going to boil down to a simple bit of blackmail. Funny how things turn out, isn't it?'

'It is.'

There was a loud ping from the kitchen.

'Dinner is served,' said Jane.

'Got any mango chutney?' asked Dixon.

'Don't push your luck.'

They were half way through their microwaved chicken tikka masalas when Dixon's phone rang. Jane listened to Dixon's end of the conversation.

'Hi Roger . . . what?'

Silence.

'Nothing at all?'

Silence.

'Well, thank you for trying.'

Silence.

'Yes, we must. OK.'

Dixon rang off.

'Don't tell me. No evidence of foul play on Georgina Harcourt's body?' asked Jane.

'None. It doesn't mean there wasn't foul play, of course, just that there's no evidence of it.'

'So, what happens now?'

'File to the coroner. Verdict suicide.'

'But you're not convinced?'

'When I was at school I got hold of a small bottle of whisky. I drank the lot and was really ill. I mean really ill. I didn't wake up till the next day. Point is, ever since then I've hated whisky. Even the smell of it makes me want to puke. So, if I was going to take an overdose I'd hardly wash it down with Scotch, would I? I'd just throw the pills up again.'

'And she hated whisky?'

'You heard what Stockman said.'

'So what do we do?'

'Let it go. We'd never get Lewis to authorise a murder investigation on this evidence.'

'True.'

'Fight your battles where you can win them, Jane,' said Dixon. 'Fancy a DVD?'

'No.'

———

Dixon sat up in bed. Jane was fast asleep. He checked the time. 2.15 a.m. Red wine always did this to him, particularly when mixed with painkillers. He looked around the room. Light from the street lamps was streaming in around the curtains. He could make out the dressing table, wardrobe and Monty asleep on the end of the bed. He could hear a police siren in the distance and remembered why he had moved to a little cottage in the country. Peace and quiet. Until two men break in at the dead of night, that is.

He lay back, closed his eyes and tried to go to sleep. He saw his handwritten list of mobile phone calls Noel made to and received from the unregistered pay as you go number. The calls began a year ago, just at the time Noel found his new meal ticket. Dixon thought about the dates of the calls. Irregular and often weeks apart.

He sat bolt upright in the bed. Jane woke up and tried to pull the duvet back over her shoulders.

'What is it?'

'Where's your laptop?'

'In the drawer under the coffee table. What . . . ?'

Dixon had already jumped out of bed and was running into the living room. Jane put her dressing gown on and followed him.

'What's the matter?'

'Just a theory.'

'A theory? You get me out of bed at this time in the morning for a theory?'

Dixon was powering up Jane's laptop.

'What's your password?'

'There isn't one.'

'Tea would be nice,' said Dixon, smiling.

Jane went into the kitchen and put the kettle on. Dixon turned back to the laptop, opened a web browser and went to racingpost.com. He typed 'Westbrook Warrior' into the search field and hit 'Enter'. Two results appeared immediately under the search tab. HORSES (1) and GREYHOUNDS (1). Odd name for a greyhound, thought Dixon. He clicked on HORSES (1) and beneath that appeared the entry 'Westbrook Warrior (IRE) – 2010'. Dixon clicked on it and a new window opened. It contained Westbrook Warrior's complete race record.

Dixon jumped up and ran into the bedroom. He picked up his jacket and found the handwritten list of calls in the inside pocket. Then he sat back down in front of the computer and checked the dates of the races against the dates of the calls.

They were a perfect match.

Chapter Ten

'S he's late.'

'You did say 8 a.m.'

'Did I?' asked Dixon, shaking his head. He looked at his watch. It was 7.45 a.m.

DCI Lewis stood in the doorway of Dixon's office.

'I got clearance on the mobile positioning. The request went in last night. Should be through today.'

'Thank you, Sir,' said Dixon, without looking away from his computer. 'Any news on the . . . ?'

He looked up. Lewis had gone.

'Marvellous.'

'What happens now?' asked Jane.

'See if you can find Louise's notes on the owners, will you?'

Jane went outside to Louise's desk in the CID room. Dixon opened Internet Explorer on his computer and went to racingpost.com. He entered 'Westbrook Warrior' into the search field, clicked on his name in the results and then went to his race record, which opened in a new window, as before. At the top of the page was the information he was looking for. Owner B & M Mayhew, S & J Somerville, Lady Winton.

'Found anything?'

'Not yet,' replied Jane.

'Find out when Hesp started training Westbrook Warrior, then.'

'How do I do that?'

'Use your initiative.'

Jane took her phone out of her handbag and rang Kevin Tanner. Dixon listened to her end of the conversation.

'Mr Tanner, it's Detective Constable Winter.'

Silence.

'I was hoping you could answer a simple question for me.'

Silence.

'When did Mr Hesp start training Westbrook Warrior?'

Silence.

'Thanks . . . yes, that's it. Thanks again.' Jane rang off and turned to Dixon.

'A year ago, when he came over from Ireland.'

Dixon nodded.

'What are you thinking?' asked Jane.

'Morning, all,' said Louise, from the doorway.

'Perfect timing,' said Dixon. 'Come in and sit down. Saves me going through it twice.'

Louise sat at Janice Courtenay's desk.

'What's going on?' she asked.

'We have some progress, which narrows it down for us. Where are your notes on the owners, Louise?'

'Bottom drawer of my desk.'

'OK. We know from Freer that roughly eighteen months ago Noel started appearing in the car park on the A39 again and on a fairly regular basis. We also know that he had a regular client. Right?'

'Yes,' said Jane.

'Then about a year ago he stopped going so often. Freer tells us that Noel said he no longer needed the money . . .'

'He had a new meal ticket.'

'He did, Louise.'

'This coincides almost exactly with the start of the telephone calls passing between the unregistered pay as you go and Noel's phone. Not only that but the dates of the calls, leaving aside the close season . . .' Dixon paused, '. . . exactly match the dates of Westbrook Warrior's races.'

'Shit.'

'Precisely, Jane.'

'Now we find this morning that Hesp began training Westbrook Warrior a year ago, when the horse came over from Ireland. We can check the exact dates, of course . . .'

'So, what d'you think happened?' asked Louise.

'Noel has a regular punter. An anonymous suit. Noel knows nothing about him, not even his name. All he knows is the car he drives, of course. Then one day, a year or so ago, this suit turns up at Gidley's Racing Stables with his shiny new racehorse and meets the groom . . .'

'Noel.'

'Yes. Now, let's say this proud new racehorse owner is accompanied by his wife and perhaps the other members of the syndicate too?'

Jane and Louise were both nodding.

'You can just see the cogs going round in Noel's head, can't you?'

'You can,' said Louise.

'Which makes Noel's new meal ticket one of Westbrook Warrior's owners?'

'It does, Jane.'

'I'll get the file,' said Louise, jumping up from her chair.

'It really is blackmail, then,' said Jane, shaking her head.

'Well, he paid a heavy price for it,' replied Dixon.

'He did.'

'And we've still got to prove it.'

Louise reappeared carrying a brown file. She began sorting through the papers and produced a plastic wallet.

'These are Westbrook Warrior's,' she said, passing the documents to Dixon.

Dixon read aloud.

'Brian and Mary Mayhew, Simon and Jean Somerville. Lady Ruth Winton. Mean anything to anyone?'

'No,' said Jane.

'Not known to police,' said Louise.

'The Mayhews live in Exford, the Somervilles in Trull. Is this it?' asked Dixon, holding up three pieces of paper in his right hand.

'I'd not got to them yet,' replied Louise.

'What about Lady Winton?' asked Jane.

'Stoke Gabriel, Devon. It says here she's ninety-one. Is that right, Louise?'

'Yes.'

'OK, Jane, you take the Mayhews and, Louise, you concentrate on the Somervilles. Anything and everything you can find out about them.'

'Yes, Sir.'

'Then we'll pay 'em a visit.'

'Shall I ring them?' asked Jane.

'No. We'll go unannounced,' replied Dixon.

Westbrook House, Trull, was set back off the road with ornate stone pillars and large wrought iron gates at the entrance. They were open. Jane turned into the drive and followed it around to the right, parking directly in front of the property, next to a silver Land Rover Discovery.

'Not short of a bob or two, are they?' said Jane.

Dixon looked up at the house. It was whitewashed with black painted timber framing over an open porch. Bay trees stood in pots on either side and, under cover, large stacks of firewood had been stored within reach of the front door. A Virginia Creeper covered the wall to the left of the porch.

'No.'

Dixon rang the doorbell. It was a small white plastic box stuck onto the door frame. It had a soft grey rubber button and a green light flashed when he pressed it.

'I hate these bloody things. You can never tell whether it's rung or not.'

They waited. No sound came from inside so Dixon knocked on the front door. This time they could hear dogs barking at the side of property, closely followed by shouting. A woman's voice.

'Come here. Pepper, come . . . oh, for heaven's sake.'

Monty was barking and scrabbling at the side window of Dixon's Land Rover. Dixon and Jane turned just in time to greet two black Labradors. The dogs began jumping up at them just as the woman appeared.

'I'm so sorry about that,' she said, hooking her fingers in the dogs' collars. 'They're quite friendly, just a bit bouncy.'

'That's fine,' said Dixon. 'We're looking for Mrs Jean Somerville.'

'That's me. And you are?'

'Detective Inspector Dixon and Detective Constable Winter, Avon and Somerset Police. May we have a word, please?'

'What about?'

'We're investigating the death of Noel Woodman, Westbrook Warrior's groom.'

'Wasn't that an accident?'

'No,' replied Dixon.

'Oh. You'd better come round the back. The kitchen door's open.'

'Is your husband in?'

'He's down at the orchard, tidying up. Do you want me to get him?'

'We'll have a word first, if that's OK.'

They followed Mrs Somerville around the side of the property. She was crouched over with her fingers still hooked in the dogs' collars, and once in the back garden she let them go. Dixon looked along the back of the property. A timber framed conservatory stuck out into the lawn and beyond that was a large bay window.

'What a lovely garden,' said Jane.

'Thank you. Mowing the lawn was a bit of a pain till I bought my husband a sit on mower. Tremendous fun.'

The back door was open.

'Come in. Do sit down,' said Mrs Somerville, gesturing towards the kitchen table. 'I'll be back in a moment.'

Dixon turned to Jane.

'Notice the uniform?' he whispered.

'What?'

'Blue Barbour jacket, green wellies, Burberry hat.'

'Tweed on race day?' asked Jane.

'Guaranteed.'

Mrs Somerville reappeared. The hat and coat had gone, revealing long grey hair tied up in a bun, grey pullover and jeans. Dixon estimated that she was in her early sixties.

'Cup of tea?'

'That would be lovely,' replied Dixon, 'thank you.'

Jean Somerville spoke while she filled the kettle. Jane was taking notes.

'So, if it wasn't an accident, what happened to him?'

'He was murdered,' said Dixon, matter of fact.

'You're not serious?'

'Perfectly.'

'Who? Why?'

'We were hoping you might be able to help us with that.'

'You don't think that I . . . we . . . had anyth . . . ?'

'There are certain questions we have to ask everyone, Mrs Somerville,' replied Dixon. 'Procedure.'

'Of course.'

'Tell me about Lady Winton.'

'She's my aunt. Housebound now, but loves to watch him run on the television. Keeps her going, I think, following the racing.'

'And your husband. What does he do for a living?'

'Retired now, but he was a property developer.'

'Did either of you have much to do with Noel?'

'Not really. We saw him at the races and on the odd occasion we went to Spaxton, but that's it.'

'Ever see him outside racing?'

'No.'

'So, you weren't friends?'

'Certainly not.' Indignant.

'Let's start at the beginning, then,' said Dixon. 'When did you buy Westbrook Warrior?'

'Just over a year ago. Simon and Brian—Brian Mayhew—went over to Tattersalls Ireland and bought him. They brought him back and put him with Michael Hesp.'

'Why Hesp?'

'We wanted a local trainer so we could keep in touch with him, and he had a vacancy.'

'Was Noel working there at that time?'

'Yes. We were there when the Warrior arrived in the lorry and so was Noel.'

'Tell me what happened.'

'When we brought him over?'

'Yes.'

'Not much to tell, really.' She laughed to herself. 'It was a bit embarrassing. He was going berserk in the lorry. Put a couple of dents in the side of it. No one would go in and untie him. So Noel went in. Calm as anything, untied him and led him down the ramp.'

'Is the Warrior aggressive?'

'He can be.'

'But not with Noel?'

'No.'

'They had a special relationship?'

'They did.'

'Didn't you think it a bit odd, then, that the Warrior kicked him to death?'

'I did, to be honest.'

'Did you say anything to anyone?'

'Only to . . .'

'Can I help?'

Dixon and Jane looked over to the back door. A green Barbour jacket, this time, and green wellies.

'Simon, this is the police. They're asking about the groom, Noel.'

'What about him?'

'He was murdered, Sir.'

'Murdered? You're joking, surely?'

'No, Sir. How well did you know him?' asked Dixon.

'Hardly at all. We saw him on race days but that's about the extent of it.'

'Did you ever see him anywhere else?'

'No.'

'How would you describe Westbrook Warrior's temperament?'

'No one could go in his stable, that's for sure. I tried it once and only just got out in one piece. And he gives the farrier a hell of a time, by all accounts. Vicious little . . .'

'What about Noel?'

'What do you mean?'

'Tell me about his relationship with Westbrook Warrior. Did he go in his stable, for example?'

'No one did, unless he was tied up. That was the golden rule.'

'And his results?'

'We expected better, I think it's fair to say.'

'Have you ever tackled Michael Hesp about them?'

'Once or twice. He fobbed us off with some rubbish about false splints.'

'Splints?' asked Dixon.

'It's damage to the splint bone in the lower leg. It causes a bony lump to form.'

'I've felt his leg. There are no splints,' said Mrs Somerville.

'We'll be changing trainer as soon we can,' said Mr Somerville.

'I think you will,' said Dixon.

Mrs Somerville handed Dixon and Jane a mug of tea each and then placed a sugar bowl on the table.

'Thank you,' said Jane.

'You've told me about Lady Winton. What about Mr and Mrs Mayhew?'

'We've known them for years . . .' said Mrs Somerville.

'Brian and I worked together for many years before I retired. Property development, that sort of thing. He's still at it but I got out before the crash. More through luck than judgement, I might add.'

'What sort of developments?'

'What do you mean?'

'Big, little . . . ?'

'The biggest we did was one hundred and twenty houses on the edge of Taunton. He's into some even bigger stuff now, though.'

'Right, well, thank you for your time,' said Dixon. 'We'll be in touch again in due course.'

'What for?'

'Just routine, Mr Somerville. And thank you for the tea.'

'I'll drive,' said Dixon, as they walked back around the side of Westbrook House to his Land Rover.

'Are you . . . ?'

'I'll be fine. No painkillers today.'

Jane passed him the keys.

'What did you make of that?' asked Jane, as soon as the car door slammed shut.

'Their reactions seemed genuine enough, but I'm wondering who Mrs Somerville spoke to about Noel's death.'

'Quite.'

'There's another conversation to be had there. And preferably when the bloody husband is out.'

Jane nodded.

'Let's get over to Exford,' said Dixon.

The drive from Trull had taken a little under an hour but Dixon had always loved Exmoor and enjoyed the trip, despite the heavy rain. He looked across to Dunkery Beacon but it was shrouded in low cloud. Jane was on her mobile phone, talking to Louise, but her signal went as they dropped down Church Hill into Exford.

'Useless thing. She was about to say something about Mayhew.'

Jane looked up at the White Horse as they drove through the village. 'Looks nice.'

'We'll pop in there for lunch on the way back,' replied Dixon.

Dixon followed the road over the bridge and up out of Exford. The river beneath the bridge was a raging torrent of water.

'What river is that, I wonder?' asked Jane.

'Well, given that this is Exford, the River Exe would be a shrewd guess,' replied Dixon.

Jane rolled her eyes.

The road climbed steeply out of the village, forcing Dixon to change down into first gear. The Land Rover lurched forward and the gearbox screeched in protest. Monty woke up in the back and started barking.

'Would you like me to drive?' asked Jane.

Dixon glared at her.

He made a sharp right turn before continuing the steep climb up to the moor itself. Jane's phone rang just as he turned into the entrance to Ferndale House.

'Voicemail,' said Jane, listening to the message. 'That was Louise. It seems that Mr Mayhew sits on the Exmoor National Park Authority planning committee. He's also a magistrate and sat on the old Police Authority before it was disbanded.'

Dixon smiled. 'Well, let's get it over with.'

'D'you think he knows we're coming?'

'Yes.'

Ferndale House was surrounded by trees, giving it some protection from the open moorland weather. It was sideways on to the road, two thirds of the way up the hill, overlooking Exford in the valley below. Dixon could see various outbuildings and stables, which appeared empty. A black BMW four wheel drive was parked outside the garage off to the left.

Dixon rang the doorbell.

'Nobody could miss that,' he said.

'No barking,' said Jane. 'Fancy living out here and not having a dog.'

'There are some very strange people about, Jane.'

Dixon heard footsteps on a tiled or stone floor. Then fumbling with the lock. The door opened to reveal a woman in her late fifties. She had dyed hair and wore no makeup. Her eyes were bloodshot and Dixon noticed that she was carrying a large glass of white wine.

'Yes?' Her speech was slurred.

'Mrs Mary Mayhew?'

'Who are you?'

'Detective Inspector Dixon and Det . . .'

'My husband's in his office.'

'Is that here or elsewhere?'

'Here. Follow me.' Mrs Mayhew was holding on to the door to stop herself swaying from side to side.

'Actually, we'd like a word with you first, if we may?'

'What about?'

'May we come in?'

She stood to one side, allowing Dixon and Jane into the hall.

'This way.'

She opened the door to her left and stepped into the drawing room. Dixon and Jane followed.

'We're investigating the death of Noel Woodman.'

'Who's he when he's at home?' Mrs Mayhew was standing by the fireplace holding onto the mantelpiece.

'Westbrook Warrior's groom.'

'Bloody horse kicked him . . .'

'He didn't, actually.'

'What do you mean?'

'Noel was murdered.'

'You're joking, surely.'

Dixon waited. Mary Mayhew was swaying backwards and forwards.

'How?' she asked.

'I'm afraid I can't reveal that at the present time.'

'At least the bloody horse didn't do it, I suppose. There was me thinking it was our fault somehow.'

'How well did you know him?'

'Hardly at all.'

She took a large swig of wine from the glass and then collapsed into a small chair to the left of the fireplace.

'Are you all right, Mrs Mayhew?' asked Jane.

'You want to try living out here. It may look nice but it's . . .'

'Inspector Dixon?'

Dixon turned around to see a man standing in the doorway.

'Mr Mayhew?'

'Yes. Simon told me you were coming. Please forgive my wife. It's usually mid-afternoon before she's in this state. It must be the weather.'

'Piss off.'

'Come through to my office, will you?'

Dixon and Jane followed Brian Mayhew along the hall. Dixon looked back at Mrs Mayhew before he left the drawing room. She was sitting with her eyes closed, tears streaming down her cheeks. He looked into the kitchen as he walked past and spotted an open bottle of wine on the kitchen table. It was half empty.

Brian Mayhew was dressed casually. Green corduroys, a brown cardigan and carpet slippers. His office was large. The curtains were closed and the room was dark. Mayhew switched on the light.

'Sorry, I was on my computer.'

Dixon surveyed the room. It had a large desk with red leather inlay. The computer was a Mac, top of the range, or so Dixon thought. There were several oil paintings on the walls, all of race-horses, and various trophies on the mantelpiece. The open fire had not been lit. Dixon's eyes were drawn to a gold mobile phone on Mayhew's desk.

'Please sit down,' said Mayhew, gesturing to the red leather chairs in front of his desk. 'Simon tells me the groom was murdered?'

'He was.'

'How?'

'Tradition dictates that I ask the questions and you answer them, Mr Mayhew,' said Dixon.

'Yes, of course. Sorry.'

'Did it surprise you to learn that Westbrook Warrior kicked him to death?'

'I thought you just said . . .'

'I did. I'm asking about your initial reaction.'

'Oh, I see. No, not really. The Warrior can be aggressive. We all knew that. That's why Hesp put in place strict procedures.'

'But the horse had a special relationship with Noel, didn't he?'

'To an extent, yes. He still had to be careful, though.'

'Did Westbrook Warrior ever kick Noel, as far as you are aware?'

'You'd need to ask Hesp that. I really don't know.'

'How well did you know him?'

'Woodman?'

'Yes.'

'Hardly at all, really. He was Hesp's employee. I don't mix with the staff.'

'Had you ever met Noel before?'

'No.'

Mayhew leaned forward and moved his computer mouse from side to side.

'Did you ever see him outside the horse racing setting?'

'No. Look what's this all about?'

Dixon ignored him.

'You're a property developer, I gather?'

'Yes.'

Mayhew's mobile phone rang and the screen lit up. The ringtone reminded Dixon of the bell in an old fashioned Bakelite telephone. Mayhew answered it.

'I'll call you back, Matt. I've got somebody with me at the moment.'

Mayhew rang off.

'What have you been working on recently?' asked Dixon.

'We're just coming to the end of a two hundred house development.'

'Where?'

'Torbrook Meadow. It's between Glastonbury and Street.'

'How long's that been going on?'

'Two years, nearly.'

'How often do you visit the site?'

'It varies. Not so much lately. More to begin with, but once it's up and running I hand it over to project managers and start looking for the next one.'

'Have you found a next one?'

'On the edge of Wiveliscombe. Look, what's this all about?'

'Just routine, Sir,' replied Dixon.

'Well, I don't like it.'

'Where were you in the early hours of Thursday 7th November?'

'Right, that's it. Get out.' Mayhew stood up sharply. His chair shot backwards, crashing into a small drinks cabinet. Several bottles fell on the floor.

Dixon stood up. He looked down at Mayhew's mobile phone on the desk, next to his computer.

'Is that real gold?' he asked.

'Of course it isn't,' replied Mayhew. 'Now get out of here.'

Dixon and Jane followed Mayhew back along the hall to the front door. Mrs Mayhew was still in the drawing room, asleep in the chair, although Dixon felt sure that she would have been woken up by the noise of the door being slammed behind them. He turned to Jane and grinned.

'Let's try that pub.'

———⌣———

'What the hell was all that about?'

'What d'you mean?'

'You practically accused him of killing Noel . . .'

'I wanted to see his reaction.'

'Why?'

They were sitting in the corner of the lounge bar in the White Horse, by the fire. Dixon had a pint of Exmoor Stag and Jane a lager shandy. They had both ordered fish and chips.

'Ring Louise and tell her to get full accounts for Mayhew's companies. Last three years. Details of all directors and shareholders too. And I want to know about Torbrook Meadow. Everything. Tell her to start from when the first planning application went in.'

Jane opened her handbag and took out her iPhone.

'No signal,' she said. 'What are you thinking?'

'Where is Torbrook Meadow?'

'Glastonbury.'

'How long's he been working on it?'

'Two years, he said, didn't he?'

'Probably longer, then, with all the planning applications.'

Jane nodded.

'He's living in Exford, working in Glastonbury. Talk me through his journey home,' said Dixon.

'Well, he'd go along the A39 to the M5 . . .' Jane stopped midsentence. 'The A39!'

'The A39. Right past the car park.'

'We've got him.'

'Let's not get too carried away. Somerville would go that way to Trull as well, if he's had anything to do with Torbrook Meadow.'

'We need to get hold of Louise.'

'We do.'

Dixon was deep in thought.

'Stop picking at your food,' said Jane.

'Yes, Mother.'

'What's the matter?'

'I don't know. Something's bugging me but I can't put my finger on it.'

Suddenly, Dixon stopped eating and looked at Jane.

'What?'

'Give me your mobile phone,' he mumbled through a mouthful of food.

Jane took her iPhone out of her handbag and passed it to Dixon.

'What network are you on?'

'O2, why?'

Dixon looked at the top left corner of the screen. It was empty, confirming that Jane had no signal. He took his own iPhone out of his inside jacket pocket and looked at it. In the top left corner was a graph, three bars rising to the right, indicating a partial signal.

'I've got a signal,' he said.

'What network are you on?' asked Jane.

'Orange. It's not a full signal but . . .' His voice tailed off.

'What's up?'

'Eat up, we have to go.'

They arrived back at Bridgwater Police Station just before 3.30 p.m. Jane had got a signal as they climbed out of Exford and had rung ahead with the list of information and documents they needed.

Louise was waiting for them with a pile of documents three inches thick, including full company searches, accounts, director and shareholder records, planning applications and estate agents sales particulars.

'Well done, Louise.'

'Thank you, Sir.'

'Right, go through that lot and see if you can find any reference to Simon Somerville playing any part in the development at Torbrook Meadow.'

'Yes, Sir,' replied Louise.

'Thinking about it, do a company search on the selling agents. See if Somerville's a director there too.'

Dixon went into his office and shut the door. Then he sat down in front of his computer and checked his email. Nothing of interest except one from Roger Poland attaching the photograph of the faint square outline around the shoe imprint on Noel's body. Dixon didn't open it. Instead he opened Internet Explorer and went to Google.

He entered 'gold mobile phone' into the search field and hit the 'Enter' button. Then he clicked on 'Images' and began scrolling through pages and pages of photographs of gold phones. Nothing. He scrolled back to the search field and changed the keyword to 'gold mobile phone nokia'. He hit the 'Enter' button again and began scrolling through more photographs of gold phones, this time all Nokia models. Several looked similar but none matched Brian Mayhew's phone. He was about to give up when the phone rang on his desk.

'Dixon, you got a minute?'

'Yes, Sir.'

Dixon locked his computer and then opened his office door. Jane looked up.

'Another summons,' said Dixon.

Jane nodded.

Dixon walked along the corridor and knocked on the door to DCI Lewis' office.

'Come in.'

DCI Lewis was sitting behind his desk. DCI Bateman was pacing up and down in front of the window. He was not in uniform.

'What the bloody hell's going on, Dixon?' said Bateman.

Silence.

'Well?'

'Don't tell me. I rattle Mayhew's cage, so he rattles your cage. Then you rattle mine. And round we go again.'

Lewis struggled to stifle a laugh.

'No, we don't go round again. Have you any idea who he is?'

'How can I put this politely, Sir? I don't give a flying fuck who he is . . .'

'How dare . . .'

'And thank you, Sir.'

'What for?'

'Confirming my suspicions.'

Dixon turned round and walked out of Lewis' office, slamming the door behind him.

'What was that all about?' asked Jane.

'Mayhew pulling strings.'

Dixon stormed into his office and slammed the door behind him.

'Steady on.'

'Sorry, Janice. Didn't see you there.'

'Bateman?'

'Yes.'

'I wondered what he was doing up here.'

Dixon turned back to his computer and unlocked the screen. Then he began scrolling through the images of gold Nokia mobile phones again. His finger hovered over the 'Close' button in the top right corner of his screen.

He froze.

There it was. A picture of the exact phone that Brian Mayhew had. Dixon clicked on the link. The screen changed to a close up of the phone. Next to it was the model name and number. Dixon reached for a pen and scribbled it on the palm of his hand. Nokia Asha 310. He stared at the enlarged image on the monitor in front of him. In the top left corner of the screen were two graphs, rather than one. Next to the first was the number one on a white square and next to the second was the number two, again on a white square. Both graphs were complete indicating two full signals.

Dixon closed the 'Image' search and went back to the Google Web search. He entered 'Nokia Asha 310' and hit the 'Enter' button. The first result came from nokia.com. Dixon read aloud.

'Nokia Asha 310 Dual Sim, browse faster, be social . . .'

Dixon turned and sat staring out of the window of his office. He heard the telltale ping of an email arriving. He opened it. The body of the email was blank but the title said it all, 'Good for you!' It came from DCI Lewis.

Dixon smiled. Then he jumped up from his desk and ran to the door.

'Louise, have those mobile positioning records arrived yet?'

'I've forwarded them to you. They'll be in your inbox.'

Dixon heard another ping from his computer behind him. He sat down and opened the attachment to the email. It was a spread-sheet giving dates, times, mobile base station code numbers and grid references for both Noel's phone and the unregistered pay as you go number. Dixon picked a grid reference for the unregistered number at random and entered it into gridreferencefinder.com. It was two miles south of Wincanton racecourse. Next he checked the date on racingpost.com. Westbrook Warrior managed third in the Thomas Lucy Novice Hurdle. He checked another. And another.

'Louise.'

'Yes, Sir.'

'We need mobile positioning records for Brian Mayhew's personal number. The same dates as we've got for the unregistered pay as you go. OK?'

'But . . .'

'No buts. Drop everything and get it organised now, please.'

Dixon could hear Louise typing.

'I've sent an email to DCI Lewis, Sir.'

'Thank you.'

Dixon began counting. He had reached nine when the phone rang on his desk.

'I'm on my way, Sir,' he said.

⌣

'Well?'

'Noel was blackmailing Mayhew, Sir.'

'Go on.'

'The unregistered pay as you go is Noel's punter.'

'How do you know that?'

'The calls began a year ago just after Freer tells us that Noel had found a new meal ticket.'

'I've read his statement.'

'This is the same time that Westbrook Warrior went to Hesp's racing stables and the calls all took place on days Westbrook Warrior was racing.'

Lewis nodded. Dixon continued.

'Not only that but the mobile positioning of the unregistered number puts the caller within a few miles of the racecourses too . . .'

'So, why Mayhew?'

'I got a look at his phone today. It's a Nokia Asha 310. The important bit is that it's dual SIM.'

'Dual SIM?'

'It has two SIM cards in it at the same time. And two SIM cards means two numbers.'

'His own and the unregistered pay as you go?'

'Yes. These mobile positioning records may not be that accurate in rural areas, but if they are identical for both numbers, it proves that both SIM cards were in the same phone at the same time.'

'And then we've got him.'

'We have, Sir.'

'Leave it with me, Nick.'

<hr />

'No mention of Somerville anywhere here, Sir,' said Louise.

'We've been through the lot,' said Jane.

'OK. Nothing much is going to happen until the morning now so you head off, Louise. Be back here at 8 a.m. sharp, please.'

'What's the mobile positioning about?' she asked, as she stood up.

'Mayhew's phone is a Nokia Asha 310.' Dixon paused. 'Dual SIM.'

'Two SIM cards in it?'

'That's right. And if the mobile positioning on his own number matches the unregistered pay as you go, they're in the same phone . . .'

'And we've got him,' said Louise.

'We have.'

Louise grinned. 'See you in the morning, then,' she said, picking up her handbag.

'Give me five minutes, Jane, and we'll head off.'

'But it's only 5 p.m.'

'No matter. I'm not sitting here for the sake of it.'

Dixon checked his email and then switched off his computer. He stretched his left shoulder and waited for the pain to course through it. Nothing.

'Shoulder feels a bit better.'

'Good. C'mon, let's go if we're going,' said Jane.

'You drive,' said Dixon, passing the keys to Jane.

They drove north out of Bridgwater on the A38, through Pawlett where it all began only a week before, and into Burnham. Jane parked in the car park in front of the Royal Clarence Hotel. It was bright moonlit night and the moon added to the lights from the Pavilion. They gave Monty ten minutes on the beach and then sat in the corner of the lounge bar.

'Did you check your email?' asked Jane.

'Yes.'

'Did you see the one from Roger?'

'Yes. But I didn't look at the photo.'

Jane took a folded piece of paper from her handbag and gave it to Dixon. He unfolded it and found himself looking at a colour copy of the mark on Noel's upper back.

'It's faint because of his clothes but can you see the square outline . . . ?' Jane pointed to it.

'I see it,' said Dixon.

'What do you think it is?' asked Jane.

Dixon stared at the photograph. He turned it first sideways and then upside down. The outline framed the imprint of the horseshoe almost exactly, except there was no line across the base of the shoe, just the sides and front.

'No idea,' he said.

'Think back to Mayhew's office . . .'

'What?'

189

'The trophies on his mantelpiece . . .'

'Cricket?'

'Yes.'

'You think it's a cricket bat?' asked Dixon.

Jane nodded.

He looked at the photograph again. Then he took out his phone and rang Roger Poland.

'Hi, Roger, thanks for the photo,'

'No problem.'

'Listen, our main suspect plays cricket and Jane has a theory that the shoe was nailed to a bat . . .'

'Best explanation I've heard. Nailed to the bottom of a cricket bat. Fits perfectly.'

'So, it's possible?'

'Very likely, I'd say. I'll do some measurements tomorrow and let you know.'

'Thanks, Roger.'

Dixon rang off.

'Well done, Jane.'

They were back at Dixon's cottage by 7.30 p.m.

'We forgot there's no telly,' said Jane.

'Let's get an early night. Either way, it's going to be a long day tomorrow.'

Chapter Eleven

Dixon was up by 4.30 a.m. He couldn't sleep, his mind going over and over the possible outcomes that lay ahead. He was standing in the kitchen, looking out across the fields at the back of his cottage, both hands clamped around a mug of tea.

If the mobile positioning of Brian Mayhew's phone matched the unregistered pay as you go then it would be a simple matter of arresting him and searching Ferndale House from top to bottom. That computer would need a thorough going over, he thought. And finding a cricket bat with nail holes in the bottom would be too good to be true.

If it didn't match, then he was back to square one. Almost. It was still going to be either Mayhew or Somerville, but which one?

Or Hesp. Fuck. He'd ruled Hesp out on the basis that the Albanians would have dealt with Noel if it had been the betting or the drugs he was threatening to blow the whistle on. But what if it was Hesp in the car park all along?

Why hadn't he thought of that? He opened the kitchen cupboard, took out a box of Tramadol and threw it in the bin. Bloody painkillers. That was his excuse and he was sticking to it.

He looked down at his feet. Monty was sitting on the floor next to him. Dixon leaned forward over the sink and looked up at the night sky through the kitchen window. It was clear.

'C'mon, matey, let's get some fresh air.'

They walked out of Brent Knoll towards Berrow, Monty on his extending lead. Dixon thought about Hesp and his alibi for the night of Georgina Harcourt's apparent suicide. A married woman in Taunton. He made a mental note to get it checked first thing in the morning.

What about the other racehorse owners? He shook his head. None of the other horses raced on all of the same days as Westbrook Warrior. A few overlapped, but none had raced at all of the same meetings Westbrook Warrior competed at.

By the time he reached the Berrow Triangle, he had convinced himself he was on the right track. And Brian Mayhew's reaction confirmed it. Now it was down to the mobile positioning to settle it.

Dixon noticed a For Sale board nailed to the Berrow Inn pub sign. Shame. He walked down the side of the pub, through the turnstile and across the golf course to the beach. The path veered off to the right but Dixon took the direct route, straight across the fairways. Once on the beach, he let Monty off the lead, and sat on an old tree stump that had been washed up. He'd been sitting there for several minutes before he realised that he was close to the spot where Valerie Manning's headless body had been found in a burnt out car only a few weeks before. Unwelcome images began to flash across his mind. Time to go.

He was walking back across the golf course when his phone rang. It was Jane.

'Where are you?'

'Out with Monty. I'm on my way.'

'Hurry up. We've got to be going soon.'

Dixon looked at his watch. It was 6.30 a.m. and still dark.
'I'll be twenty minutes or so.'

Louise was waiting for them when they arrived at Bridgwater Police
Station.

'DCI Lewis was looking for you, Sir.'

'What did he want?'

'I got the impression he's getting a bit jumpy about going after
Brian Mayhew,' said Louise. 'He was asking what else we've got on
him apart from the phones.'

'What did you tell him?'

'That he'd need to speak to you.'

'The right answer. Well done, Louise.'

'What else have we got?'

'Nothing . . . yet,' replied Dixon. 'Remind me of the name of
Hesp's alibi for the night Georgina Harcourt died, will you?'

'Miriam Sims,' said Jane.

'Let's check it out. The two of you can go. Take Louise's car.
And be discreet. Remember, she's married.'

'What do we do if her husband answers the door?'

'Use your imagination, Jane.'

'Yes, Sir.'

'And see if the husband was away for any of Westbrook
Warrior's races.'

'Yes, Sir.'

Dixon sat down at his desk and switched on his computer. The
system was painfully slow, so he had time to get a coffee from the
machine before the computer booted up. He checked his email.
Nothing. Then he opened Internet Explorer and searched Google
Images for 'horse saddles'. It was a bewildering array of different

types, shapes and colours, some leather and some synthetic. He went back to Google, entered 'horse saddle design' into the search field and hit the 'Enter' button. As usual, Wikipedia came to his rescue and he spent the next hour reading about the various designs and their uses. By the end of it, he was far from an authority on the subject but he did, at least, understand the different types of saddle.

DCI Lewis had been standing in the doorway of Dixon's office for nearly a minute before he coughed loudly.

'Sorry, Sir, didn't see you there.'

Lewis closed the door behind him and sat down on the chair in front of Dixon's desk.

'I've spoken to Collyer.'

Dixon nodded. 'And . . . ?'

'They've got nothing that might assist. Let's leave it at that, shall we?'

'No, we shan't leave it at that. That doesn't tell me anything. They might have nothing but then they might have information but be refusing to reveal it.'

'They've got nothing. Take it from me. Look, if this goes any further . . .'

'What?'

'It's a telephone tap. That's all they've got in there, and apart from the call asking for you on the Sunday evening, there's nothing.'

'Well, at least we know,' said Dixon. 'Thank you, Sir.'

'The request for the mobile positioning went in last night. Expedited. The chief super took some convincing.'

'About the expense involved or Brian Mayhew?'

'Both,' replied Lewis. 'You'd better be right about him or we're both going to look like idiots.'

'That will be a new experience for me, Sir.'

'And me, you cheeky sod.'

'What time will the records get here, do we know?'

'Lunchtimeish,' replied Lewis. 'Where are Jane and Louise?'

'Gone to speak to Hesp's alibi for Sunday night.'

'Does he need an alibi for a suicide?'

'I want to know if the relationship is genuine.'

'Why?'

'Because he's less likely to be hanging around in car parks if it is.'

'Mayhew is married, isn't he?'

'In name only by the looks of things.'

'Well, keep me posted. I can let you have Dave and Mark now if you need them.'

'Thank you, Sir.'

Dixon took Monty for a walk in Victoria Park and was just putting him back in the Land Rover when Jane and Louise pulled into the car park.

'Well?'

'Do I look like an Avon lady?' asked Jane.

'Do I have to answer that?' replied Dixon.

'The husband answered the door. It was the best I could come up with on the spot . . .' said Louise.

'Anyway, he left us to it in the lounge and went back to bed. He'd got home late last night, apparently.'

'And?'

'Hesp was there, and is regularly when her husband is away.'

'Did you check the dates?'

'He was away for several of Westbrook Warrior's races, yes.'

'Good.'

'What happens now?' asked Louise.

'We wait.'

___

Dixon was just finishing a cheese sandwich from the canteen when he heard the familiar ping of an email arriving. He took his feet off the windowsill, sat up and swung his chair round to face his computer. The email came from cellsiteanalysis.net. It was the one he had been waiting for.

He opened it and clicked on the attachment. A large Excel spreadsheet opened on the screen in front of him. Then he opened the file on his desk and took out a paper copy of the mobile positioning spreadsheet for the unregistered pay as you go phone that had been used to speak to Noel in the days and weeks before his murder.

Dixon could feel himself shaking. His hands felt stone cold to the touch yet he was sweating. Profusely.

He checked the dates, times, mobile base station codes and coordinates for the unregistered pay as you go on the paper spreadsheet against the same data for Brian Mayhew's phone number on the screen in front of him.

An exact match.

'Gotcha.'

The unregistered pay as you go SIM card had been in Brian Mayhew's gold Nokia Asha 310 when the calls were made to and received from Noel Woodman.

And Mayhew had lied.

Dixon jumped up from his desk and ran to the door of his office.

'Jane.'

'Yes, Sir.'

'We've got him. Get Lewis.'

Jane abandoned her coffee in the machine and ran along the corridor to DCI Lewis' office. Dixon looked at his watch. It was just after 12.30 p.m. He sat back at his desk, minimised the spreadsheet and then opened Internet Explorer. He went to racingpost.com and looked at the racecard for Taunton that day. Westbrook Warrior was going in the 2.05 p.m., the Batstone Financial Management Handicap Chase.

DCI Lewis appeared in the doorway of Dixon's office. Jane and Louise were standing behind him.

'The mobile positioning for Mayhew's phone is an exact match, and I mean an exact match, each and every entry, with the pay as you go number,' said Dixon.

'You've got him,' said Lewis.

'We have, Sir.'

'Well, go and pick him up.'

'There's a slight complication there . . .'

'What?'

'He'll be at Taunton for the 2.05 p.m. Westbrook Warrior's racing today.'

'He's gonna miss the race, then, isn't he?' said Lewis.

'I'll need Dave and Mark . . .'

'No problem.'

'And we'd better have a car either side of the racecourse to block the road when we pick him up. Just in case.'

'The Taunton lot can do that. Leave it with me.'

'Thank you, Sir.'

Dixon looked past DCI Lewis to Jane.

'Get me Noel's phone from the evidence store, will you?'

'Yes, Sir.'

'And check it's charged up.'

Dixon spent five minutes on the Taunton Racecourse website while he waited for Jane. He looked at the enclosure guide and familiarised himself with the layout. It was a clear, crisp autumn day with a blue sky and plenty of sunshine. Unless he was sitting down to lunch, Mayhew would be in the Owners Viewing Enclosure at the far end of the Portman Stand. Wearing tweed, binoculars in hand, no doubt.

Dixon could hear Dave Harding and Mark Pearce talking to Louise outside his office. Then Jane arrived back from the evidence store with Noel's phone.

'Right then,' said Dixon, 'this is Brian Mayhew.' He handed photographs to each of them.

'*The* Brian Mayhew?'

'Yes, Dave. D'you know him?'

'Know of him. I've never met him.'

'Good,' replied Dixon. 'We're arresting him on suspicion of the murder of Noel Woodman. He'll be at Taunton Racecourse watching his horse run in the 2.05 p.m.'

'Why don't we just pick him up when he gets home?' asked Pearce.

'We pick him up at the first opportunity, Mark. This is a murder investigation, remember. And what if he doesn't go home?'

Mark Pearce nodded.

'It's a fine day so he'll probably be in the Owners Viewing Enclosure for the race. Either that or having lunch in the restaurant.'

'I'd be watching the race,' said Louise.

'So would I,' replied Jane.

'Uniform will be blocking the road either side of the course in case he makes a run for it. But there'll be no uniform on the course itself. Just us.'

'What about an ambulance, Sir?' asked Harding. 'Just in case . . .'

'There'll be one on the course, anyway, so we'll be all right on that score,' replied Dixon.

DCI Lewis walked across the CID Room and stood behind Jane.

'I've been onto the Taunton lot and there'll be a patrol car either side of the course on the B3170 and another blocking the car park. Let them know via radio when you're moving in and they'll block the road.'

'Thank you, Sir,' replied Dixon.

'Good luck.'

'Anyone familiar with the course?'

'I am,' said Harding.

'Good. For those of you who aren't, there are three grandstands. First on the left as you go in is Paddock. That's where the restaurant is. Louise, you can go in and see if you can find him.'

'Yes, Sir.'

'Second on the left is the Portman Stand. At the far end of that is the Owners Viewing Enclosure. The last stand is Orchard but I can't see why he'd be in there, although he could be in the Betting Ring, which is in front of it.'

'Or the private boxes. And there are hospitality suites too,' said Harding.

'They're between the last two stands. If we can't find him anywhere else, we can look in there, Dave. Good thinking. Just keep your eyes peeled and we'll soon spot him.'

'Who'll be with him?'

'His wife, probably. Mary Mayhew. And possibly also Simon and Jean Somerville.'

'Who are they?' asked Pearce.

'Friends and co-owners,' replied Dixon. 'Right, everyone clear what's going to happen?'

'Yes, Sir.' In unison.

'Keep in touch by radio and sing out if you see him. Keep a low profile, though. I don't want to draw attention to ourselves unnecessarily. The idea is to get him out of there nice and calm. OK?'

'Yes, Sir.'

⸻

They sped south on the M5 to Taunton, getting off at Junction 25 and then cut around the back of the Blackbrook Business Park, before turning south east out of Taunton on the B3170 towards the racecourse. They passed a patrol car parked in a farm gateway, ready and waiting to block the road. Just inside the entrance to the car park, directly opposite the racecourse, was another patrol car.

Dixon and Jane, with Louise, Dave Harding and Mark Pearce following, turned into the car park. They were greeted by a marshal wearing a fluorescent jacket. He directed them to the furthest field, at least two hundred yards away. Dixon presented his warrant card.

'We need to be near the entrance.'

'There isn't room, I'm afraid.'

'Make room.'

'Park behind those two cars over there. They're ours. I'll move the cones.'

'Thank you,' said Dixon.

He parked in a small section just inside the entrance and off to the right. Dave Harding parked next to him.

Dixon looked around. Every other car seemed to be a four wheel drive, and several of them were black. He spotted a large BMW.

'Wait here.'

He jogged over to a gap in the hedge, jumped the large puddle in the middle, and then ran along the hedge towards two cars parked side by side in the next field. A silver Land Rover Discovery and a black BMW X5. He walked back.

'They're here. That's the Somervilles' Discovery too.'

Dixon looked at his watch. It was 1.30 p.m. He could hear the on course commentator announcing the runners and riders for the 1.35 p.m.

'We'll wait here until the next race starts and then go in quietly. Dave, you and Mark head for the far end. Hang around the Betting Ring.'

'Yes, Sir.'

'We'll try the restaurant first in the Paddock Stand, Louise, and then work our way along.'

Dixon reached into the glove box of his Land Rover and put his binoculars in his pocket. Jane rolled her eyes.

'Not for the horses, Constable. I'll need them to spot Mayhew.'

'Yes, Sir,' replied Jane, smiling.

Dixon tapped on the window of the patrol car and showed his warrant card to the officer in the driver's seat.

'Wait until you get the signal and then just park across the gateway so no one can get out.'

'Yes, Sir.'

Dixon listened to the on course commentary coming over the tannoy system. The 1.35 p.m. was under starter's orders. He reached into his inside jacket pocket and checked Noel's phone one last time. It had 31 per cent battery left. That would do.

'C'mon, everyone, let's get it over with.'

They followed Dixon across the road, past the ticket window, and waited while he spoke briefly to the elderly gentlemen on the turnstile. They could see Dixon showing the men his warrant card before being waved through. Once inside, Harding and Pearce walked straight across the concourse in front of the grandstands to the far end.

Dixon looked to his right. He could see the white rails stretching away into the distance and spotted a group of horses on the far side of the course. Brightly coloured silks moving in a clockwise direction. According to the on course commentator, All But Grey was ten lengths clear coming to the final bend before the home straight.

The terraces of the Paddock Stand to his left were raised up and enclosed by glass at the front, offering protection from the weather for the owners, trainers and members. Dixon, Jane and Louise walked along the front of the stand, hidden from view. They stopped near the entrance.

'In you go, Louise. See if you can see him.'

Dixon watched the 1.35 p.m. finish directly in front of them, the finishing line marked by a small white painted wooden tower opposite the Portman Stand. As predicted, All But Grey crossed the line well clear of the rest of the field.

Louise reappeared in the doorway. She was out of breath.

'He's not in there. I checked the restaurant and the stand.'

'You're sure?' asked Dixon.

'Yes.'

They continued along the front of the Paddock Stand to the corner. Dixon noticed the first aid room off to his left, in between the end of the Paddock Stand and the Portman Stand, which was now directly in front of them. It was now almost deserted, the spectators having made for the Betting Ring in readiness for the next race. Dixon took out his binoculars and scanned the on course bookmakers for any sign of Mayhew. He could see Dave Harding and Mark Pearce wandering around. He could also see J Clapham Racing at the far end. No sign of Mayhew.

The Winner's Enclosure to their right was now a hive of activity. Grooms were holding the winning horse and the owners were being presented with a trophy by the chairman of Barton Building

Services, according to the tannoy system. Dixon looked back in the direction of the Parade Ring. He could see Westbrook Warrior, Hesp and Tanner but no sign of Mayhew, or the Somervilles for that matter.

'Where the hell are they?' asked Jane.

'Get up there and have a look in the bar behind the viewing area there, Louise,' said Dixon, gesturing towards the Portman Stand.

Louise ran up the concrete terraces of the Portman Stand, along the front and in the door to the bar. Dixon listened to the commentator giving the starting prices for the 2.05 p.m.

'Westbrook Warrior's the favourite,' said Jane.

Dixon looked at the odds on the big screen opposite the grandstands, in the centre of the course. Westbrook Warrior was at the top of the list. Three to two. Noel would have been proud.

He looked at his watch. Ten minutes to go to the start of the race. A small crowd had gathered on the rails just behind the finishing line. There was a crossing point there at the end of the Betting Ring where it was possible to walk across the course to the central area. The rail had been slid back, allowing access, and a few people had done so. Dixon looked at them through his binoculars. No sign of Mayhew or the Somervilles.

Louise came running down the terraces of the Portman Stand.

'He's not in there either.'

'Ring Dave and get him to check the Orchard Stand. There's a restaurant in the back too, I think.'

Jane rang Dave and passed on the instructions.

Dixon watched the horses in the Parade Ring to his right. They were getting ready for the start of the 2.05 p.m. Westbrook Warrior was the biggest by some margin. His jockey wore green and gold stripes and certainly looked the part. Dixon missed the announcement of Best Turned Out but thought it could well have been the Warrior.

He could see the horses that had run in the 1.35 p.m. in the Unsaddling Enclosure, being washed down and rugged up.

'They look bloody tired,' he said.

'So would you if you'd just run two miles,' said Jane.

'True.'

Dixon waited for a call from Dave Harding. The on course commentator announced that the horses were making their way out to the start on the far side of the course. The Betting Ring began to clear as the spectators started to make their way back to the terraces to watch the race. Dixon could see a marshal sliding the rail back into place, blocking off the crossing point. He passed the binoculars to Jane.

'Keep an eye out for Mayhew.'

Jane began scanning the spectators standing along the rail. Her phone rang.

'That was Dave. No sign.'

'Shit.'

'*They're under starter's orders . . .*'

'For fuck's sake.'

'There they are,' shouted Jane.

'*They're off.*'

'Where?' asked Dixon.

The commentator was in full flow, following the race. '*Westbrook Warrior's on the rail, two lengths clear as they come to the first flight . . .*'

'They've come out of the hospitality suites and are walking across to the rail over there,' said Jane, pointing.

Dixon looked through the binoculars. He saw Mayhew walking with his wife, Mary, towards the crossing point. He was carrying a glass of champagne and she a glass tumbler, probably a gin and tonic. Both were wearing tweed. They were arm in arm and presented a picture of marital bliss, which struck Dixon as odd. Appearances can be deceptive, he thought. Or was it something else?

'Jane, let Dave and Mark know, will you? Tell them to stand clear off to the left at the end of the Betting Ring.'

Jane took out her mobile phone.

'Louise, tell uniform to block the road and the car park.'

'. . . *and as they come past the grandstands for the first time, Westbrook Warrior is five lengths clear from Daytime Blues and Gladbig in third . . .*'

Dixon heard the pounding of the horses' hooves and looked across to see them go past. He could hear the spectators along the rail, the Mayhews included, shouting encouragement.

'Dave and Mark are moving in,' said Jane.

'And the road's blocked,' said Louise.

'Right, you two over by the finishing post there. That tower thing. And make sure they don't see you, Jane.'

'Yes, Sir.'

'Let's do it, then.'

Dixon walked quickly across the concourse towards Brian and Mary Mayhew. They were leaning on the outer rail, drinks in hand. Dixon could see Dave and Mark on the rail to their left. Jane and Louise were by the finishing post to the right.

'. . . *with one circuit still to go, Westbrook Warrior is now ten lengths clear of Gladbig in second . . .*'

Dixon stood five paces directly behind Mayhew. He waited.

'. . . *as they come past the grandstand for the final time, Westbrook Warrior is twenty lengths clear of the field and looking comfortable . . .*'

He could hear the Mayhews cheering as Westbrook Warrior went past. What had struck Dixon as odd before now hit him square in the face. Mary Mayhew was no more drunk now than she had been when they met her at Ferndale House. Half a bottle of wine on the kitchen table. It had been a convincing act. He wondered who the driving force of the marriage was as he reached for Noel's phone and rang the unregistered pay as you go number.

Dixon could hear the phone ringing in Mayhew's pocket only a few paces in front of him. The ringtone was different. No bell this time. Instead, Dixon recognised the default Nokia ringtone.

Brian Mayhew was leaning over the rail and looking to his right, waiting for Westbrook Warrior to come off the bend in the distance and onto the home straight for the final time. The blood drained from his face. Mary Mayhew stared at his jacket pocket as he took the phone out and looked at the screen. Dixon could see Brian Mayhew's hand shaking as he placed the phone to his ear. Mayhew looked at his wife. He opened his mouth to speak but said nothing. He shook his head. Mary Mayhew appeared frozen to the spot.

Dixon rang off. Mayhew turned to his right and looked straight at Dixon. Mary Mayhew turned to her left and saw Dixon. Her face contorted into a picture of pure hatred. She turned back to her husband, who was still staring at Dixon. In one movement, she smashed her glass on the rail to her right and thrust the broken piece into the left side of her husband's neck. Then she twisted it.

Blood began pumping from Brian Mayhew's neck. He dropped his glass and clutched his throat with both hands. Mary Mayhew stepped back as Brian Mayhew dropped to his knees and fell backwards. Blood began pouring from his mouth as he coughed and spluttered. Dixon took his jacket off and ran forward. He shouted across to Jane.

'Get an ambulance. And the first aider.'

'. . . *as they come off the final bend Westbrook Warrior is sixty lengths clear with two flights to go . . .*'

He wrapped his jacket around Mayhew's neck in an attempt to stem the flow of blood. Mayhew was gurgling and crying at the same time. Air bubbles formed in the blood in his mouth. Each time he coughed, Dixon was sprayed with blood as he held his jacket around Mayhew's neck.

Dave Harding arrived.

'It's got the carotid artery, Dave. Hold this and see if you can stem the flow.'

'. . . *Westbrook Warrior lands the final hurdle still sixty lengths clear . . .*'

Dixon looked over his shoulder. Mary Mayhew had disappeared. He saw movement to his right. She had gone under the rails and was standing on the course directly in Westbrook Warrior's path as he came up on the stand side. Her arms were outstretched, tears streaming down her face.

Dixon looked back down the course. Westbrook Warrior was no more than a hundred yards away and going full pelt for the finish line. Dixon ducked under the rail, ran forward and threw himself on Mary Mayhew. Both of them crashed to the ground. Mary Mayhew was lying face down. Dixon was lying on top of her. He could hear the thunder of Westbrook Warrior's hooves as the horse approached.

Dixon closed his eyes and put his hands over his head. He could hear the on course commentator in the distance and Mary Mayhew sobbing. He felt the ground vibrating beneath him, as the horse got nearer. Then silence. He opened his eyes and looked to the right just in time to see a pair of aluminium racing plates sailing over his head. He waited. Westbrook Warrior landed on the other side.

'Good lad,' thought Dixon.

He looked back down the course. The chasing pack was still over a hundred yards away. Dixon took his chance. He jumped up, grabbed Mary Mayhew by the coat and dragged her back under the railings. They got clear by the narrowest of margins just as Gladbig crossed the line in second place.

Dixon fell back onto the tarmac concourse. He looked up. A crowd had gathered around the scene. He could see Dave Harding standing over Brian Mayhew. He looked at Dixon and shook his head. Jane ran over and handcuffed Mary Mayhew.

'Mary Mayhew, I'm arresting you on suspicion of the murder of Brian Mayhew . . .'

'And Noel Woodman,' said Dixon.

'He was blackmailing him. And Brian was too spineless to do anything about it.'

When she spoke, the image of a cobra spitting venom flashed across Dixon's mind. He nodded to Jane.

'Mary Mayhew, I'm arresting you on suspicion of the murders of Brian Mayhew and Noel Woodman. You do not have to say anything but it may harm your defence if you do not mention when questioned something that you later rely on in court. Anything you do say may be given in evidence.'

'I told him I'd kill him if his sordid little secret ever came out. He laughed at me. Well, he's not laughing now, is he?'

More venom.

A siren drowned out the on course commentary.

'Ambulance's on its way, Sir,' said Jane.

'Bit late,' replied Dixon. 'Get her out of here.'

'Yes, Sir.'

Mark Pearce and Louise led Mary Mayhew away to a waiting police car. Jane helped Dixon to his feet.

'What the bloody hell were you playing at?'

'A horse will never tread on a human if it can avoid it, Jane,' said Dixon, brushing the mud off his trousers.

'How d'you know that?'

'Saw it on a John Wayne film once. Can't remember which one.'

'Idiot.'

'Thank you, Constable.'

'How's the shoulder?'

'Fine.'

They watched as Brian Mayhew was placed on a stretcher and the blanket pulled over his face. The paramedics carried him over to the waiting ambulance.

'He never even got to see his horse win,' said Dave Harding.

'What on earth is going on?'

Simon and Jean Somerville were trying to push through the crowd, which was being dispersed by uniformed officers and racecourse marshals.

'What's happened to Brian and Mary?'

'Sort them out, will you, Dave?'

'Yes, Sir.'

⎯⎯⎯ ⌣ ⎯⎯⎯

Dixon looked over to where Brian Mayhew had died. The white railings were dripping with blood and the sand on the crossing was stained deep red. He had seen too much bloodstained sand recently.

The tannoy crackled into life.

'Ladies and gentlemen, we regret to announce that due to an incident, racing for the day is abandoned. Please make your way home safely and your tickets will remain valid for the next meeting. Thank you.'

Dixon sat on the metal steps leading up to the finishing post. He was covered in mud and blood. Jane sat next to him.

'I've got the local lot getting names and addresses.'

'Good thinking,' said Dixon. 'There'll be no shortage of witnesses.'

'Plenty of camera footage as well, don't forget,' said Jane.

Dixon shook his head.

'Fancy dying live on Channel 4 . . .'

Chapter Twelve

Dixon and Jane arrived back at Bridgwater Police Station to find a large crowd gathered around the television in the corner of the CID Room. They were watching the BBC News Channel. Nobody noticed them arrive, so they crept into Dixon's office and closed the door. Dixon leaned back in his chair in the dark and closed his eyes.

There was a knock at the door.

'Staying out of the limelight?' asked DCI Lewis, switching on the light.

'I don't feel much like celebrating, Sir.'

'Why not? It's all over the TV news . . .'

'It was an arrest that went wrong . . .'

'Rubbish. How could you possibly have known his own wife was going to do that?'

Dixon looked out of the window. He had known Mary Mayhew had not been as drunk as she made out when he had met her at Ferndale House the day before. And the marital bliss at the racecourse had been an act. But that was it. He turned back to DCI Lewis.

'I didn't know she was going to do that, no.'

'There you are, then. Don't beat yourself up about it.'

'Thank you, Sir.'

Dixon knew he wouldn't do that. But he still didn't feel like celebrating either.

He spent the afternoon interviewing Mary Mayhew. She confessed to both killings, which made for a short interview, at least as far as double murders go. It had not been the money. What Noel had demanded was 'small change', as she put it. No, she had suffered what she regarded as the ultimate betrayal by her husband, with public humiliation soon to be heaped on top, and she had exacted her revenge. Dixon got the distinct impression that she found the public humiliation the harder to bear. And she was clearly proud of what she had done.

A thorough search of Ferndale House was undertaken that same afternoon. A horseshoe and the charred remains of a cricket bat handle were found in an old oil drum used for burning garden rubbish at the bottom of the orchard, just as Mrs Mayhew had said they would be. Brian Mayhew's computer had been seized and was on its way to the High Tech Unit for examination.

It was just after 5.30 p.m. when Mary Mayhew was charged with the murders of Noel Woodman and Brian Mayhew. Dixon was surprised when she began to sob as the charges were read to her by the custody sergeant. Perhaps the full implications of what she had done had hit home. No more horse racing and champagne.

Dixon and Jane watched her being led back to the cells.

'But for a chance meeting in the Zalshah, she'd have got away with it,' said Jane.

'And Brian Mayhew would still be alive . . .'

'You heard what Lewis said?'

'I did.'

'What do we do now?' asked Jane.

'Exeter Prison.'

'Jon Woodman?'

'I've got to tell him that his brother wasn't a well intentioned whistleblower after all. Just a blackmailer.'

'Nice.'

'Give me five minutes.'

Dixon sat at his desk and rang DCS Collyer. Voicemail. Dixon left a message.

'This is Nick Dixon, Sir. Bridgwater CID. We talked about the horse lorries at Gidley's Racing Stables being used to import drugs. On the roof of the large blue one is a storage box. It's full of spare saddles, according to Hesp. But they're not racing saddles. Racing saddles are flat pads. These are old dressage and jumping saddles. You'll find the drugs stitched into the panels.'

Dixon stood in the doorway of his office.

'There are going to be sixteen racehorse owners looking for a new trainer very soon.'

Jane smiled.

'C'mon, let's get out of here.'

Two days later, Dixon was sitting at home flicking through the channels on his new television. He had a new DVD player too but, much to Jane's relief, had not yet replaced his film collection.

'I'm off to see my parents. Back about fiveish,' said Jane.

'OK,' replied Dixon, without looking away from the screen.

He continued flicking through the channels and landed on 'Channel 4 Racing'. He watched the 12.35 p.m. from Haydock, followed by the 12.50 p.m. from Lingfield. He looked at Monty sitting on the sofa next to him.

'What d'you think, matey?'

Dixon reached for his laptop and powered it up. Then he opened Internet Explorer and logged in to Bet29.com.

He could feel his credit card burning a hole in his back pocket.

About the Author

Damien Boyd is a solicitor by training and draws on his extensive experience of criminal law, along with a spell in the Crown Prosecution Service, to write fast paced crime thrillers featuring Detective Inspector Nick Dixon.

Made in the USA
Monee, IL
10 April 2020

25506354R00129